MW01240508

World Builder

By Lashelle Alee

First published 2013, third edition published 10/20/22

Table of Contents

Table of Contents

Table of Contents

Introduction

Are you an author, a gamer, a playwright, or simply a person whose active imagination immerses you into a world that is unlike our own? Have you ever dreamed of a faraway planet filled with life you can't find on Earth? Or perhaps you've experienced moments of enlightenment about what might exist beyond our realm, ideas that beg you to elaborate and share with others around you? This book is the perfect resource for anyone who wants to build their own world in such vivid detail that it comes to life in the minds and hearts of others.

Everyone has good ideas. Great ideas, on the other hand, are a rarity. The difference between the two is often that a great idea is the combination of many good ones blended seamlessly together. Many people believe all you need is one spark of creativity to elicit interest, but to turn that interest into fascination, you must use that concept only as a starting point. This book is a guide that will allow you to take your good ideas and transform them into exceptional ones.

World Builder is filled with questions to make your fantasy something you can see, hear, smell, taste, and feel. Take each question as you envision it and answer according to your need. You may come across questions you don't immediately know the answer to. It's okay to skip those, as you can always complete them later if you desire. If you need more room for your ideas, be sure to use the notes pages included at the end of each section.

There are several online and print resources for world building that may serve as a reference for topics outlined in this book. Often, however, you may find that your best ideas will strike you in everyday life. By taking a minute to stop and ask yourself "what if?" you will free your mind from the restraints of the real world, opening it to limitless alternative possibilities.

Sit down and finish this book all at once or fill in the blanks only as needed. No matter how you choose to go about it, one truth will remain the same; eventually you will know every crucial detail about your setting, and you will have unlimited story telling possibilities.

Discover your world so thoroughly that others doubt reality in favor of fiction. Grab a pen and start your journey now!

Additional Works

If you enjoy this book, stay tuned for more books in the Builder Series, including:

- City Builder

- Religion & Mythos Builder

- Bestiary Builder

- Plant Compendium Builder

I am also working on a children's series of books with kid appropriate creative exercises such as imaginative prompts, fill-in-the-blanks, and coloring.

Please sign up for my mailing list at www.lashellealee.com to be notified when my new books launch.

Thank you for your support!

The Basics

What is your world's name? If it is known by several names, list all of them.

_____

_____

Draw your world's symbols.

What is the mood or theme of your world?

_____

_____

_____

Describe your world in three words.

_____   _____   _____

What is the most interesting thing about your world?

_____

_____

_____

How similar is your world to Earth?

_____

_____

_____

The Basics

Describe your world's basic planetary information.

Size	
Gravity	
Year Length	
Day Length	
Hours of Light in a Day	
Hours of Dark in a Day	

Describe the elemental composition of your planet.

%	
%	
%	
%	
%	

Draw your world from space.

What constellation is your world a part of?

_____

What galaxy is your world a part of?

_____

What makes up the atmosphere surrounding your planet?

_____

_____

_____

How is your planet shifting or changing?

_____

_____

_____

Describe the process and effects of your planet's growth.

_____

_____

_____

Describe your world's age:

Newborn   Young   Mid-Age   Old   Ancient

Describe your world's growth:

Shrinking   Stable   Expanding

Describe your world's average technical aptitude:

Primitive   Pre-Industry   Post-Industry   Advanced   Futuristic

Describe the magical essence of your world:

Non-Magical   Poor   Average   Rich

The Basics

Describe your world's suns and moons.

Name: Sun   Moon

Notes:

Name: Sun   Moon

Notes:

Name: Sun   Moon

Notes:

Name: Sun   Moon

Notes:

Name: Sun   Moon

Notes:

Notes on the Basics

The Universe

How old is the universe?

_____

How was the universe created?

_____

_____

_____

What is the age of your world by the records of its inhabitants?

_____

How was your world created?

_____

_____

_____

What events or elements influenced the shaping of your world?

What significant changes has your world experienced over time?

_____

_____

_____

What significant changes are expected to affect your planet in the future?

_____

_____

_____

Draw the sky in the dark hours of the night as seen from your world.

Draw the sky in the light hours of the day as seen from your world.

The Universe

List the names of a few notable galaxies.

1.	6.
2.	7.
3.	8.
4.	9.
5.	10.

List the names of a few notable constellations.

1.	6.
2.	7.
3.	8.
4.	9.
5.	10.

Draw one or more constellations.

Notes on the Universe

Geography & Climate

How many continents are in your world?

_____

How many continents have been discovered and by who?

_____

List the names of your continents.

1. _____	9. _____
2. _____	10. _____
3. _____	11. _____
4. _____	12. _____
5. _____	13. _____
6. _____	14. _____
7. _____	15. _____
8. _____	16. _____

How many islands are in your world?

_____

How many islands have been discovered and by who?

_____

List the names of a few notable islands.

1. _____	7. _____
2. _____	8. _____
3. _____	9. _____
4. _____	10. _____
5. _____	11. _____
6. _____	12. _____

Draw or paste a map of your world's continents and islands.

Geography & Climate

Describe the frequency of your world's geographical landforms. (3 is Highest)

Mountains	0 1 2 3	Deltas	0 1 2 3
Volcanoes	0 1 2 3	Swamps	0 1 2 3
Hills	0 1 2 3	Marshes	0 1 2 3
Plateaus	0 1 2 3	Rivers	0 1 2 3
Mesas	0 1 2 3	Estuaries	0 1 2 3
Valleys	0 1 2 3	Tributaries	0 1 2 3
Plains	0 1 2 3	Gulfs	0 1 2 3
Deserts	0 1 2 3	Bays	0 1 2 3
Basins	0 1 2 3	Islands	0 1 2 3
Oceans	0 1 2 3	Peninsulas	0 1 2 3
Seas	0 1 2 3	Coral Reefs	0 1 2 3
Lakes	0 1 2 3	Glaciers	0 1 2 3
	0 1 2 3		0 1 2 3
	0 1 2 3		0 1 2 3
	0 1 2 3		0 1 2 3
	0 1 2 3		0 1 2 3
	0 1 2 3		0 1 2 3
	0 1 2 3		0 1 2 3

List the names of a few notable landforms of your world.

Feature   Location

1.

2.

3.

4.

5.

6.

7.

8.

Draw or paste a map of your world with the notable features marked.

Geography & Climate

What is the hottest place in your world?

_____

What is the coldest place in your world?

_____

What are the different climates in your world?

1. _____   5. _____

2. _____   6. _____

3. _____   7. _____

4. _____   8. _____

Describe a few of your world's climates.

Name: _____   Location: _____

Notes: _____

_____

_____

Name: _____   Location: _____

Notes: _____

_____

_____

Name: _____   Location: _____

Notes: _____

_____

_____

Name: _____   Location: _____

Notes: _____

_____

What causes your world's seasons?

_____

_____

_____

Describe a few of your world's seasons.

Name: Length:
_____
Location: Frequency:
_____
Notes:
_____
_____

Name: Length:
_____
Location: Frequency:
_____
Notes:
_____
_____

Name: Length:
_____
Location: Frequency:
_____
Notes:
_____
_____

Name: Length:
_____
Location: Frequency:
_____
Notes:
_____
_____

Name: Length:
_____
Location: Frequency:
_____
Notes:
_____
_____

Geography & Climate

Describe your world's weather. How stable or erratic is it?

_____

_____

_____

What kinds of unique and extreme weather exist? How common are these?

_____

_____

_____

Weather Phenomena for Reference*

Clouds	Storm Clouds	Wind & Dust
Noctilucent Cloud	Arcus	Cyclone
Nacreous Clouds	Asperitas Clouds	Derecho
Cirrus Clouds	Skypunch	Dust Devil
Cirrocumulus Clouds	Funnel Cloud	Dust Storms
Cirrostratus Clouds	Lenticular Clouds	Haboobs
Altocumulus	Mammatus Clouds	Gale
Altostratus	Pyrocumulus Cloud	Microburst
Nimbostratus		Monsoon
Cumulonimbus	**Precipitation**	Sandstorms
Cumulus	Blizzard	Squall
Stratus	Hailstorm	Tornado
Stratocumulus	Ice Storm	Waterspout
	Rainstorm	Hurricane
	Sleet Storm	Hypercane
	Snowstorm	Volcanic Ash
		Whirlwind
		Windstorm

*Special thanks to https://www.otherworldlyincantations.com/weather-features-fantasy-worldbuilding/ for this inclusive list. Visit this page for images and descriptions!

Slides & Floods

Avalanche

Flood

Landslide

Lava Flow

Mudslide

Dryness, Heat, & Fire

Drought

Firestorm

Fire Whirl

Heat Wave

Wildfire

Cold & Vapor

Cold Snap

Fog

Freezing Fog

Ice Fog

Mist

Sea Smoke

Lightning & Thunderstorms

Ball Lightning

Cloud-to-Cloud Lightning

Cloud-to-Ground Lightning

Ground-to-Cloud Lightning

Catatumbo Lightning

Supercell

Thundersnow

Volcanic Lightning

How have your world's inhabitants adapted to its weather?

_____

_____

_____

_____

Are there areas of your world that are inhospitable due to weather?

_____

_____

_____

_____

Geography & Climate

How many countries are in your world?

_____

List the names of a few countries and where they are located.

	Country	Continent
1.		
2.		
3.		
4.		
5.		
6.		
7.		
8.		
9.		
10.		
11.		
12.		
13.		
14.		
15.		
16.		
17.		
18.		
19.		
20.		
21.		
22.		
23.		
24.		
25.		

Draw or paste a map of your world with the countries marked.

Geography & Climate

How many cities are in your world?

_____

List the names of a few cities and where they are located.

City	Country
1.	
2.	
3.	
4.	
5.	
6.	
7.	
8.	
9.	
10.	
11.	
12.	
13.	
14.	
15.	
16.	
17.	
18.	
19.	
20.	
21.	
22.	
23.	
24.	
25.	

Draw or paste a map of your world with the cities marked.

Geography & Climate

Describe a few of your world's notable landmarks.

Name:

Location:

Notes:

Name:

Location:

Notes:

Name:

Location:

Notes:

Name:

Location:

Notes:

Name:

Location:

Notes:

Describe a few of your world's notable landmarks.

Name:

Location:

Notes:

Name:

Location:

Notes:

Name:

Location:

Notes:

Name:

Location:

Notes:

Name:

Location:

Notes:

Geography & Climate

Draw or paste additional maps.

Draw or paste additional maps.

Geography & Climate

Draw or paste additional maps.

Draw or paste additional maps.

Geography & Climate

Draw or paste additional maps.

Draw or paste additional maps.

Geography & Climate

Draw or paste additional maps.

Notes on Geography & Climate

Accepted Principles

What is the name of your world's most accepted measurement system?

_____

Describe your world's measurements for length and distance.

Name   Description

_____   _____
_____   _____
_____   _____
_____   _____
_____   _____

Describe your world's measurements for liquid and volume.

Name   Description

_____   _____
_____   _____
_____   _____
_____   _____
_____   _____

Describe your world's measurements for mass and velocity.

Name   Description

_____   _____
_____   _____
_____   _____
_____   _____
_____   _____

Describe your world's measurements for temperature and humidity.

Name   Description

Describe your world's measurements for time.

Name   Description

Describe the measurements used in your world's most accepted calendar.

Name   Description

Are there other measurements systems present in your world? Who uses them?

Accepted Principles

What are the names of your world's "days" from its most accepted calendar?

_____   _____

_____   _____

_____   _____

_____   _____

_____   _____

What are the names of your world's "months" from its most accepted calendar?

_____   _____

_____   _____

_____   _____

_____   _____

_____   _____

Draw or detail your world's most accepted calendar.

Notes on Accepted Principles

Language

How many spoken languages exist in your world?

_____

How many written languages exist in your world?

_____

How many signing languages exist in your world?

_____

What is the dominant language of your world?

_____

List a few languages and who uses them.

	Language	Used By
1.		
2.		
3.		
4.		
5.		
6.		
7.		
8.		
9.		
10.		
11.		
12.		
13.		
14.		
15.		

Notes on Language

Religion

What is the most practiced religion in your world?

What are some of the common religious beliefs in your world?

What are some of the common religious practices in your world?

What kinds of extremist religious beliefs or cults exist in your world?

What influence has religion had on your world?

What role does religion have in magic, technology, and government?

Describe a few impactful religious events or conflicts in your world's history.

Name: _____ Date: _____

Notes: _____

_____

_____

_____

Name: _____ Date: _____

Notes: _____

_____

_____

_____

Name: _____ Date: _____

Notes: _____

_____

_____

_____

Name: _____ Date: _____

Notes: _____

_____

_____

_____

Name: _____ Date: _____

Notes: _____

_____

_____

_____

Religion

Describe a few religions that exist in your world.

Name: Worshipers Name:

Holy Symbol	Place of Worship	Religious Attire / Tool

Officials Name(s):

Deities:

Notes:

Name: Worshipers Name:

Holy Symbol	Place of Worship	Religious Attire / Tool

Officials Name(s):

Deities:

Notes:

Describe a few religions that exist in your world.

Name: Worshipers Name:

Holy Symbol	Place of Worship	Religious Attire / Tool

Officials Name(s):

Deities:

Notes:

Name: Worshipers Name:

Holy Symbol	Place of Worship	Religious Attire / Tool

Officials Name(s):

Deities:

Notes:

Describe a few notable religious figures or deities.

Religion

Name: Religion:

Notes:

Name: Religion:

Notes:

Name: Religion:

Notes:

Name: Religion:

Notes:

Name: Religion:

Notes:

Name: Religion:

Notes:

Describe a few notable religious figures or deities.

Name: Religion:

Notes:

Name: Religion:

Notes:

Name: Religion:

Notes:

Name: Religion:

Notes:

Name: Religion:

Notes:

Name: Religion:

Notes:

Notes on Religion

Religion

Notes on Religion

Magic

What is the name magic is known by in your world?

_____

Describe your world's magic system. Is it hard, with clearly defined rules or soft, vague, and undefined?

Hard Magic   Soft Magic   Combination

Where does your magic stem from?

Gods   Supernatural Forces   Elements

Items   Organic Ingredients   Rituals

Physical Energy   Mental Energy   Spiritual Energy

Words   Movements

Describe how are magical effects created.

_____
_____
_____
_____

What can magic accomplish?

_____
_____
_____
_____

What are the limitations of magic? What can it never do?

_____
_____
_____

What is the cost of magic? Who or what pays that cost?

_____

_____

_____

_____

How is magical energy replenished?

_____

_____

_____

Can anything stop or resist magic?

_____

_____

_____

Does magic have a will of its own or does it always comply with the user?

_____

_____

_____

What determines the strength and length of the magical effect?

_____

_____

_____

What happens when the magical effect ends?

_____

_____

_____

Magic

Who can use magic?

_____

_____

_____

How is magic learned? Does it come naturally or require knowledge and training?

_____

_____

_____

Are there schools, instructors, or instructions for magic? If so, describe them.

_____

_____

_____

How is magical aptitude determined? How can it be increased or decreased?

_____

_____

_____

Do different people have different magical abilities? How or why?

_____

_____

_____

Are certain magic users treated differently than others? Who and why?

_____

_____

_____

Who knows about magic, and do they understand its source?

_____

_____

_____

How is magic perceived? It is celebrated, tolerated, or persecuted?

_____

_____

_____

Who abuses magic and what do they gain?

_____

_____

_____

How long has magic been in use? Can it ever be taken away?

_____

_____

_____

What influence has magic had on your world?

_____

_____

_____

What role does magic have in religion, technology, and government?

_____

_____

_____

_____

Magic

Describe a few impactful magical events in your world's history.

Name: Date:

Notes:

Name: Date:

Notes:

Name: Date:

Notes:

Name: Date:

Notes:

Name: Date:

Notes:

Detail some of your magical abilities, spells, components, rituals, or items.

Name:	**Name:**
Notes:	Notes:
Name:	**Name:**
Notes:	Notes:

Magic

Detail some of your magical abilities, spells, components, rituals, or items.

Name:	**Name:**
Notes:	Notes:
Name:	**Name:**
Notes:	Notes:

Detail some of your magical abilities, spells, components, rituals, or items.

Name:	**Name:**
Notes:	Notes:

Name:	**Name:**
Notes:	Notes:

Magic

Detail some of your magical abilities, spells, components, rituals, or items.

Name:	**Name:**
Notes:	Notes:
Name:	**Name:**
Notes:	Notes:

Describe a few notable magic users.

Name: Period Lived:

Notes:

Name: Period Lived:

Notes:

Name: Period Lived:

Notes:

Name: Period Lived:

Notes:

Name: Period Lived:

Notes:

Name: Period Lived:

Notes:

Notes on Magic

Notes on Magic

Technology

How advanced is the technology that exists in your world?

Who has access to the most advanced technologies and why?

What influence has technology had on your world?

How is technology perceived?

What technological cataclysms has your world experienced?

What role does technology have in magic, religion, and government?

What kinds of technology exist in your world?*

Energy	Fuels, Generators, Batteries, Distribution
Materials	Mining, Synthesis, Application; Harder, Lighter, Stronger, Smarter, Larger, Smaller, Warmer
Work	Farming, Labor, Robotics, Management, Equipment
Transport	Local, Regional, Global; Personal vs Many; Supply Chains, Logistics, Waste
Imaging	Farther, Smaller, Clearer, Projections, Holograms, Surveillance, Heat, Biometrics
Biotechnology	Birth, Sexuality, Disease, Mental Health, Surgery, Drugs, Prosthetics, Genetics, Death

*Special thanks to Reddit user gmbuilder for the use of this exceptional list!

Technology

What kinds of technology exist in your world?

Information	Communication, News, Cyberspace, Intellectual Property, Interfaces, Computing, Artificial Intelligence, Simulation
Habitats	Urban vs Rural, Home, Work, Commerce, Governance; Frontiers of Space/Oceans/Subterranean
Economics	Public vs Private Ownership, Economic Systems, Class, Currency
Politics	Local/National/Global Governance, Voting Systems, Succession Systems, Rights, Equality, Unity
Culture	Art, Music, Games, Literature, Sport, Storytelling, Events, Holidays, Myths, Cyberspace
Robotics	Vehicles, Exoskeletons, Labor, Data, Warfare

What kinds of technology exist in your world?

Trans-humanism	Cybernetics, Robotics, Clones, Genetic Engineering, Artificial Life, Longevity, Mind Transfer
Warfare	Soldiers, Smart Weapons, Energy Weapons, Energy Shields, Biochemical Weapons, Stealth, Cryptography, Cyberwarfare, Long Range, Mass Destruction
Space	Detection, Propulsion, Satellites, Speed of Light, Gravity, Asteroid Mining, Terraforming, Defense
Alien Life	Detection, Defense, Language, Diplomacy, Uplifting, Hive Minds, Superorganisms
Parapsychology	Telepathy, Mind Control, Telekinesis, Pre/Post-Cognition
Alternate Dimensions	Detection, Travel, Time Travel, Simulated Reality

Technology

Describe a few technological breakthroughs that shaped your world's history.

Name: Date:

Notes:

_____

_____

_____

_____

Name: Date:

Notes:

_____

_____

_____

_____

Name: Date:

Notes:

_____

_____

_____

_____

Name: Date:

Notes:

_____

_____

_____

_____

Name: Date:

Notes:

_____

_____

_____

Detail some of your world's technologies.

Name:	**Name:**
Notes:	Notes:
Name:	**Name:**
Notes:	Notes:

Technology

Detail some of your world's technologies.

Name:	**Name:**
Notes:	Notes:
Name:	**Name:**
Notes:	Notes:

Detail some of your world's technologies.

Name:	**Name:**
Notes:	Notes:

Name:	**Name:**
Notes:	Notes:

Technology

Detail some of your world's technologies.

Name:	**Name:**
Notes:	Notes:
Name:	**Name:**
Notes:	Notes:

Describe a few notable inventors.

Name: Period Lived:

Notes:

Name: Period Lived:

Notes:

Name: Period Lived:

Notes:

Name: Period Lived:

Notes:

Name: Period Lived:

Notes:

Name: Period Lived:

Notes:

Notes on Technology

Notes on Technology

Government

Describe the frequency of governments that exist in your world. (3 is Highest)*

Democracy	0 1 2 3	Feudalism	0 1 2 3
Republic	0 1 2 3	Kritarchy	0 1 2 3
Democratic Republic	0 1 2 3	Tribalism	0 1 2 3
Federation	0 1 2 3	Timocracy	0 1 2 3
Confederation	0 1 2 3	Gerontocracy	0 1 2 3
Oligarchy	0 1 2 3	Diarchy	0 1 2 3
Aristocracy	0 1 2 3	Socialism	0 1 2 3
Theocracy	0 1 2 3	Technocracy	0 1 2 3
Plutocracy	0 1 2 3	Cyberocracy	0 1 2 3
Absolute Monarchy	0 1 2 3	Stratocracy	0 1 2 3
Constitutional Monarchy	0 1 2 3	Geniocracy	0 1 2 3
Fascism	0 1 2 3	Noocracy	0 1 2 3
Empire	0 1 2 3	Demarchy	0 1 2 3
Autocracy	0 1 2 3	Magocracy	0 1 2 3
Totalitarian	0 1 2 3	Despotism	0 1 2 3
Communism	0 1 2 3	Kleptocracy	0 1 2 3
Anarchy	0 1 2 3	Fragile State	0 1 2 3
Military Coup	0 1 2 3	Cyclical Bureaucracy	0 1 2 3

*Special thanks to https://www.chaoticanwriter.com/worldbuilding-36-types-of-government-part-1/ for this inclusive list. Visit this page for descriptions and examples!

What are the three largest governments in your world?

Name   Type

#1.

Notes:

#2.

Notes:

#3.

Notes:

What influence has government had on your world?

_____

_____

_____

What is one of the most influential ancient governments in your world's history?

_____

_____

_____

What are some of the most widely accepted laws worldwide?

_____

_____

_____

What are some of the harshest punishments administered by governments in your world?

_____

_____

_____

Describe one of your world's prison systems.

_____

_____

_____

What role does government have in magic, religion, and technology?

_____

_____

_____

_____

Government

Describe one of your world's governments.

Name: _____ Type: _____

Governing Level and Location: _____

Leader(s) and Title(s): _____

_____

_____

Are there divisions of power? What do they control and how do they cooperate?

_____

_____

_____

How are decisions made? How quickly does this happen?

_____

_____

_____

What does the government regulate?

_____

_____

_____

How are domestic conflicts handled?

_____

_____

_____

How are foreign conflicts and warfare handled?

_____

_____

_____

Describe one of your world's governments.

Name: _____ Type: _____

Governing Level and Location: _____

Leader(s) and Title(s): _____

_____

_____

Are there divisions of power? What do they control and how do they cooperate?

_____

_____

_____

How are decisions made? How quickly does this happen?

_____

_____

_____

What does the government regulate?

_____

_____

_____

How are domestic conflicts handled?

_____

_____

_____

How are foreign conflicts and warfare handled?

_____

_____

_____

Government

Describe one of your world's governments.

Name: _____ Type: _____

Governing Level and Location: _____

Leader(s) and Title(s): _____

_____

_____

Are there divisions of power? What do they control and how do they cooperate?

_____

_____

_____

How are decisions made? How quickly does this happen?

_____

_____

_____

What does the government regulate?

_____

_____

_____

How are domestic conflicts handled?

_____

_____

_____

How are foreign conflicts and warfare handled?

_____

_____

_____

Describe one of your world's governments.

Name: _____ Type: _____

Governing Level and Location: _____

Leader(s) and Title(s): _____

_____

_____

Are there divisions of power? What do they control and how do they cooperate?

_____

_____

_____

How are decisions made? How quickly does this happen?

_____

_____

_____

What does the government regulate?

_____

_____

_____

How are domestic conflicts handled?

_____

_____

_____

How are foreign conflicts and warfare handled?

_____

_____

_____

Government

Describe a few impactful government events or conflicts in your world's history.

Name: Date:

Notes:

_____

_____

_____

_____

Name: Date:

Notes:

_____

_____

_____

_____

Name: Date:

Notes:

_____

_____

_____

_____

Name: Date:

Notes:

_____

_____

_____

_____

Name: Date:

Notes:

_____

_____

_____

_____

Describe a few notable government officials.

Name: Period Lived:

Notes:

Name: Period Lived:

Notes:

Name: Period Lived:

Notes:

Name: Period Lived:

Notes:

Name: Period Lived:

Notes:

Name: Period Lived:

Notes:

Notes on Government

Notes on Government

Economy

What is the most widely accepted currency in your world?

List a few of your world's currencies and who they are used by.

	Currency	Value	Made From	Used By
1.				
2.				
3.				
4.				
5.				
6.				
7.				
8.				
9.				
10.				

Who monitors and assists with the exchange of currencies?

Who controls the majority of your world's wealth?

How commonly are trades for goods performed without the use of currency?

Describe a few common trades that occur in your world.

Item(s)		Item(s)		Currency & Value
1.	=		=	
2.	=		=	
3.	=		=	
4.	=		=	
5.	=		=	
6.	=		=	
7.	=		=	
8.	=		=	
9.	=		=	

What items are in surplus worldwide?

_____

_____

_____

What items are in demand worldwide?

_____

_____

_____

What groups are the most economically powerful?

_____

_____

_____

What groups are the least economically powerful?

_____

_____

_____

Notes on Economy

Notes on Economy

Nature

Describe the frequency of your world's plant life adaptations. (3 is Highest)

Bioluminescent	0 1 2 3	Thorny/Spikey	0 1 2 3
Poisonous	0 1 2 3	Drought Resistant	0 1 2 3
Carnivorous	0 1 2 3	Submergent	0 1 2 3
	0 1 2 3		0 1 2 3
	0 1 2 3		0 1 2 3
	0 1 2 3		0 1 2 3

What are some of the unique adaptations of plants in your world?

_____

_____

_____

_____

What are a few of the most valuable plants in your world? Why?

_____

_____

What are a few plants grown commonly as a food source?

_____

_____

What are a few plants in your world that have magical properties?

_____

_____

_____

_____

Detail some of your world's plants.

Name:	**Name:**
Notes:	Notes:
Name:	**Name:**
Notes:	Notes:

Nature

Detail some of your world's plants.

Name:	**Name:**
Notes:	Notes:
Name:	**Name:**
Notes:	Notes:

Detail some of your world's plants.

Name:	**Name:**
Notes:	Notes:
Name:	**Name:**
Notes:	Notes:

Notes on Nature

Notes on Nature

Creatures

What are some of the structural (body parts, coverings) adaptations of creatures in your world?

_____

_____

_____

What are some of the physiological (cells, chemicals, and internal processes) adaptations of creatures in your world?

_____

_____

_____

What are some of the behavioral (communication, hibernation) adaptations of creatures in your world?

_____

_____

_____

What are a few of the most valuable creatures in your world? Why?

_____

_____

What are a few creatures commonly kept as a food source?

_____

_____

_____

What are a few creatures commonly kept as pets?

_____

_____

_____

Detail some of your world's creatures.

Name:	**Name:**
Notes:	Notes:

Name:	**Name:**
Notes:	Notes:

Creatures

Detail some of your world's creatures.

Name:	**Name:**
Notes:	Notes:
Name:	**Name:**
Notes:	Notes:

Detail some of your world's creatures.

Name:	**Name:**
Notes:	Notes:

Name:	**Name:**
Notes:	Notes:

Notes on Creatures

Notes on Creatures

Intelligent Races

How many races of intelligent beings exist in your world?

Describe your world's racial hierarchy or coexistence.

Draw your world's racial hierarchy or coexistence mind map.

Which race has the highest population and why?

_____

_____

_____

Which race is the lowest population and why?

_____

_____

_____

Which race has the most conflict and why?

_____

_____

_____

Which race has the least conflict and why?

_____

_____

_____

How has racial diversity affected your world?

_____

_____

_____

What role does race have in technology, magic, religion, and government?

_____

_____

_____

_____

_____

_____

_____

Intelligent Races

Summarize each of your world's major races.

Name:	
Notes:	

Name:	
Notes:	

Summarize each of your world's major races.

	Name:
	Notes:

	Name:
	Notes:

Intelligent Races

Summarize each of your world's minor races.

Name:	
Notes:	

Name:	
Notes:	

Name:	
Notes:	

Name:	
Notes:	

Describe a few impactful interracial events or conflicts in your world's history.

Name: Date:

Notes:

_____

_____

_____

Name: Date:

Notes:

_____

_____

_____

Name: Date:

Notes:

_____

_____

_____

Name: Date:

Notes:

_____

_____

_____

Name: Date:

Notes:

_____

_____

_____

Notes on Intelligent Races

Notes on Intelligent Races

Major Race 1: _____

Basics

What do they call themselves and what do others call them?

_____

_____

_____

Describe them in three words.

_____   _____   _____

What is the most well-known fact or accepted belief about them?

_____

_____

_____

What is their most guarded secret?

_____

_____

_____

What is the most important part of their society?

_____

_____

_____

_____

Where does most of their population live?

_____

_____

Characteristics

Describe their average physical form.

_____

_____

_____

_____

_____

Draw or paste an image of their average physical form.

Major Race 1: Characteristics

Describe their ideal physical form.

_____

_____

_____

Describe their magical and technological characteristics.

_____

_____

_____

_____

Describe their physical characteristics.

_____

_____

_____

Describe their social characteristics.

_____

_____

_____

Describe their skills and abilities.

_____

_____

_____

Describe their attitude towards other races.

_____

_____

_____

Social Hierarchy

Describe their social hierarchy.

_____

_____

_____

Draw their social hierarchy.

How does an individual's or family's social status affect their daily life?

_____

_____

_____

How can an individual's or family's social status change?

_____

_____

_____

Gender Differences

Describe their genders.

_____

_____

_____

What are the physical differences between genders?

_____

_____

_____

What are the cognitive differences between genders?

_____

_____

_____

What are the perceived and societal gender differences for children?

_____

_____

_____

What are the perceived and societal gender differences for adults?

_____

_____

_____

How do members of different genders commonly interact?

_____

_____

_____

Language

What is the name of the language they speak or sign?

_____

Is the language also written?

_____

Describe how their language sounds and its basic principles.

_____

_____

_____

How and where did their language originate?

_____

_____

_____

How do they communicate with each other?

_____

_____

_____

How do they communicate with other races?

_____

_____

_____

How do they send messages near and far?

_____

_____

_____

Major Race 1: Language

Describe a few common words of their language.

Spoken / Signed Word	Written Word	Translation

Describe a few common phrases of their language.

Spoken / Signed Phrase	Written Phrase	Translation

Names

How are names chosen?

_____

_____

_____

How are names changed?

_____

_____

_____

What significance does a name have on an individual?

_____

_____

_____

How many parts are in a name?

_____

List a few first, female, or other gendered names.

1. _____   5. _____

2. _____   6. _____

3. _____   7. _____

4. _____   8. _____

List a few middle, male, or other gendered names.

1. _____   5. _____

2. _____   6. _____

3. _____   7. _____

4. _____   8. _____

Major Race 1: Names

List a few last, family, or identifying names.

1.	6.
2.	7.
3.	8.
4.	9.
5.	10.

List a few titles they can acquire.

Title	Acquired By
1.	
2.	
3.	
4.	
5.	
6.	
7.	
8.	
9.	
10.	
11.	
12.	

Describe how titles may be changed.

Describe the social impact of titles.

Religion

How important is religion in their society? Which religion dominates their culture?

_____

_____

_____

What purpose does religion serve in their society?

_____

_____

_____

What are their beliefs about the beginning of life?

_____

_____

_____

What are their beliefs about death, afterlife, and reincarnation?

_____

_____

_____

Where are how do they practice their religion?

_____

_____

_____

How tolerant of other religious beliefs are they?

_____

_____

_____

Major Race 1: Religion

Describe a few of their deities or important religious individuals.

Name:

Notes:

Name:

Notes:

Name:

Notes:

Name:

Notes:

Name:

Notes:

Name:

Notes:

Describe a few important religious teachings they follow or rituals they perform.

Name:

Notes:

Name:

Notes:

Name:

Notes:

Name:

Notes:

Name:

Notes:

Name:

Notes:

Magic

How important is magic in their society?

What influence has magic had on their society?

What purpose does magic serve in their society?

What do they call their magicians and what do their magicians call themselves?

Describe how they use magic.

Where did their magical knowledge originate?

Who can become a magician?

How are magicians educated?

_____

_____

_____

How are magicians treated in society?

_____

_____

_____

What laws, governing or religious, pertain specifically to magicians?

_____

_____

_____

How do magicians commonly interact with each other?

_____

_____

_____

What special groups of magicians exist?

_____

_____

_____

Describe the hierarchy of magicians.

_____

_____

_____

Major Race 1: Magic

Describe a few notable magicians or spells.

Name:

Notes:

Name:

Notes:

Name:

Notes:

Name:

Notes:

Name:

Notes:

Name:

Notes:

Technology

How important is technology in their society?

What influence has technology had on their society?

What purpose does technology serve in their society?

What do they call their technology, and what do others call it?

Describe how they use technology.

How much of their technology is borrowed or copied from other races?

Who can become an inventor and technology user?

Major Race 1: Technology

How are inventors and technology users educated?

_____

_____

_____

How are inventors and technology users treated in society?

_____

_____

_____

What laws, governing or religious, pertain specifically to technology users?

_____

_____

_____

How do inventors and technology users commonly interact with each other?

_____

_____

_____

What special groups of inventors and technology users exist?

_____

_____

_____

Describe the hierarchy of inventors and technology users.

_____

_____

_____

Describe a few notable inventors or inventions.

Name:

Notes:

Name:

Notes:

Name:

Notes:

Name:

Notes:

Name:

Notes:

Name:

Notes:

Government

Describe their government.

_____

_____

_____

Who can be a government official?

_____

_____

_____

Who can participate in the government?

_____

_____

_____

What influence does government have in their society?

_____

_____

_____

Describe a few impactful events in the history of their government.

Name: Date:
_____

Notes:
_____

_____

_____

Name: Date:
_____

Notes:
_____

_____

_____

List a few notable laws of their government.

Name: Date Enacted:

Notes:

Name: Date Enacted:

Notes:

Name: Date Enacted:

Notes:

Name: Date Enacted:

Notes:

Name: Date Enacted:

Notes:

Name: Date Enacted:

Notes:

Major Race 1: Government

Describe their foreign policies.

_____

_____

_____

Describe their treaties and alliances.

_____

_____

_____

Describe their rivals and enemies.

_____

_____

_____

Describe a few notable members of their government.

Name: Period Lived:

Notes:

_____

_____

_____

Name: Period Lived:

Notes:

_____

_____

_____

Name: Period Lived:

Notes:

_____

_____

_____

War

Describe their attitude towards war and physical conflicts.

_____

_____

_____

Describe how their society has been affected by war.

_____

_____

_____

Describe a few wars from their history.

Name: Time Period:
_____

Notes:
_____

_____

Name: Time Period:
_____

Notes:
_____

_____

Name: Time Period:
_____

Notes:
_____

_____

Name: Time Period:
_____

Notes:
_____

_____

Major Race 1: War

Describe a few of their weapons and armor.

Name: Material:
Notes:
_____

_____

_____

Name: Material:
Notes:
_____

_____

_____

Name: Material:
Notes:
_____

_____

_____

Describe a few famous warriors and peacekeepers.

Name: Period Lived:
Notes:
_____

_____

_____

Name: Period Lived:
Notes:
_____

_____

_____

Name: Period Lived:
Notes:
_____

_____

_____

History

How and where did they originate from?

_____

_____

_____

Briefly describe their history.

_____

_____

_____

Describe a few important events in their history.

Name: _____ Date: _____

Notes: _____

_____

Name: _____ Date: _____

Notes: _____

_____

Name: _____ Date: _____

Notes: _____

_____

Name: _____ Date: _____

Notes: _____

_____

Major Race 1: Achievements

Achievements

What do they consider their greatest achievement?

_____

_____

_____

What effect have their achievements had on the world?

_____

_____

_____

Describe a few additional achievements they have made.

Name: Date:
_____
Notes:
_____

_____

Name: Date:
_____
Notes:
_____

_____

Name: Date:
_____
Notes:
_____

_____

Name: Date:
_____
Notes:
_____

_____

Economics

What kind of currency is used?

_____

What is their currency made of and what does it look like?

_____

Who monitors and distributes their currency?

_____

_____

_____

What kind of trades can be made?

_____

_____

_____

How is their currency accepted by other races?

_____

_____

_____

Describe a few common valuations.

Item or Service	Trade or Monetary Value
1.	
2.	
3.	
4.	
5.	
6.	
7.	

Ownership System

What property can be owned?

Who can own property?

What laws and punishments exist regarding stolen and vandalized property?

What happens to property when the owner dies?

Describe slavery within your race and its impact on your world.

Cities

How many cities have they founded?

_____

Where and how were most cities founded?

_____

_____

_____

Describe a few notable cities.

Name: Location:
_____

Notes:
_____

_____

Name: Location:
_____

Notes:
_____

_____

Name: Location:
_____

Notes:
_____

_____

Name: Location:
_____

Notes:
_____

_____

Housing

In what type of building or area do they live? What is it made of?

_____

_____

_____

Describe how their homes are uniquely adapted to them.

_____

_____

_____

Describe their housing arrangements. Who lives together?

_____

_____

_____

Draw or paste a layout of a common home.

What special housing exists?

_____

_____

_____

Describe how wealth affects housing.

_____

_____

_____

Describe the furniture and items found in their homes.

_____

_____

_____

Draw or paste a layout of a special or wealthy home.

Education

Describe their educational system.

_____

_____

_____

List a few subjects that are taught.

1.	9.
2.	10.
3.	11.
4.	12.
5.	13.
6.	14.
7.	15.
8.	16.

Who are the instructors?

_____

_____

_____

Describe their special schools and educational programs.

_____

_____

_____

Who can attend school and who can obtain special education?

_____

_____

_____

Describe a few notable schools.

Name: _____ Location: _____

Notes: _____
_____
_____

Name: _____ Location: _____

Notes: _____
_____
_____

Name: _____ Location: _____

Notes: _____
_____
_____

Describe a few notable educators.

Name: _____ Period Lived: _____

Notes: _____
_____
_____

Name: _____ Period Lived: _____

Notes: _____
_____
_____

Name: _____ Period Lived: _____

Notes: _____
_____
_____

Professions

List a few common professions.

1. _____   5. _____

2. _____   6. _____

3. _____   7. _____

4. _____   8. _____

List a few necessary but uncommon professions.

1. _____   3. _____

2. _____   4. _____

How are professions chosen?

_____

_____

_____

How are professions able to be changed?

_____

_____

_____

How does an individual acquire their professional education?

_____

_____

_____

Describe a few professions and their trade or monetary earnings.

Profession	Trade or Monetary Value
1.	
2.	
3.	

Health

What is the name of their medical practitioners?

_____

Who can be a medical practitioner?

_____

How are medical practitioners educated?

_____

_____

_____

What treatments or medicines are used?

_____

_____

_____

What medical instruments are used?

_____

_____

_____

Does their medicine work on other races?

_____

Describe a few diseases, infections, or sicknesses they can be affected with.

_____

_____

_____

Diet

What does their diet primarily consist of?

How much and how often do they eat?

What utensils are used to prepare and cook food?

What methods is food prepared?

What food sources are gathered?

What food sources are grown or raised?

What food sources are hunted?

What food sources are traded?

Daily Life

Where do they eat?

_____

When are common mealtimes?

_____

Where do they sleep?

_____

When do they sleep and for how long?

_____

What and how do they breathe?

_____

_____

Where and how do they release waste?

_____

_____

Describe their mealtime practices.

_____

_____

Describe their travel arrangements.

_____

_____

_____

Clothing

What are their clothes made of?

_____

_____

_____

What do children wear?

_____

_____

_____

What do adults wear?

_____

_____

_____

What effect does gender have on their clothing?

_____

_____

_____

What accessories do they wear?

_____

_____

_____

What piercings, tattoos or other optional markings can they have?

_____

_____

_____

Describe a few outfits.

Worn By or For:

Notes:

Worn By or For:

Notes:

Worn By or For:

Notes:

Worn By or For:

Notes:

Grooming

How do they groom themselves? How often is it done?

_____

_____

_____

Where do they groom themselves?

_____

_____

_____

How do they view their grooming habits?

_____

_____

_____

How do other races view their grooming habits?

_____

_____

_____

What items are used and what habits are common for female grooming?

_____

_____

_____

What items are used and what habits are common for male grooming?

_____

_____

_____

Children

How are children treated in society?

_____

_____

_____

Who do children reside with?

_____

How are children educated?

_____

_____

_____

Where and with whom do children spend most of their time?

_____

_____

_____

What are a few special events in a child's life?

_____

_____

_____

At what age are children considered to be adolescents?

_____

Describe the experience of becoming an adolescent.

_____

_____

_____

Adolescents

How are adolescents treated in society?

_____

_____

_____

Where and with whom do adolescents spend most of their time?

_____

How are adolescents educated?

_____

_____

What are a few special events in an adolescent's life?

_____

_____

_____

At what age are adolescents considered to be adults?

_____

Describe the physical changes associated with becoming an adult.

_____

_____

_____

Describe the social changes associated with becoming an adult.

_____

_____

_____

Adults

How are adults treated in society?

_____

_____

_____

Where and with whom do adults spend most of their time?

_____

How are adults educated?

_____

_____

What are a few special events in an adult's life?

_____

_____

_____

At what age are adults considered to be elderly?

_____

Describe the physical changes associated with becoming elderly.

_____

_____

_____

Describe the social changes associated with becoming elderly.

_____

_____

_____

The Elderly

How are the elderly treated in society?

_____

_____

_____

What special treatments exist to honor the elderly?

_____

_____

Where and with whom do the elderly spend most of their time?

_____

_____

_____

What are a few special events in an elder's life?

_____

_____

_____

At what age do the elderly die?

_____

What ways exist to reverse the aging process or prolong the life of the elderly?

_____

_____

What influence do they elderly have on society?

_____

_____

_____

Etiquette

What is the proper relationship between the young and the elderly?

_____

_____

_____

What is the proper relationship between child and parent?

_____

_____

_____

What is the proper relationship between siblings?

_____

_____

_____

Describe a few examples of proper etiquette.

Situation:
_____

Acceptable Etiquette:
_____

Situation:
_____

Acceptable Etiquette:
_____

Situation:
_____

Acceptable Etiquette:
_____

Death

What ritual is performed after death?

_____

_____

_____

Who participates in the ritual?

_____

_____

_____

What happens to the corpse of the dead?

_____

_____

_____

In what ways are the dead honored or remembered?

_____

_____

_____

How does death affect society and an individual's family?

_____

_____

_____

List the most common causes of death.

1. _____ 5. _____

2. _____ 6. _____

3. _____ 7. _____

4. _____ 8. _____

Courtship & Marriage

How are potential partners selected for courtship?

_____

_____

How is courtship initiated?

_____

_____

Describe the process of courtship.

_____

_____

_____

What is it called to be married?

_____

_____

Under what governing law or ceremony can individuals marry and is it for life?

_____

_____

Describe the events that come before the ceremony and interactions between the individuals.

_____

_____

_____

Describe the marriage ceremony.

_____

_____

_____

Major Race 1: Courtship & Marriage

What are the social effects of marriage on the individuals?

_____

_____

_____

What are the social effects of marriage on the individuals' families?

_____

_____

_____

Describe the religious or government laws of marriage.

_____

_____

_____

Under what circumstances can the religious or governmental marriage laws be broken?

_____

_____

_____

What are the social effects on individuals if the religious or governmental marriage law is broken?

_____

_____

_____

If a married individual dies can the surviving partner(s) participate in a new marriage ceremony?

_____

_____

_____

Reproduction

At what age do they reach sexual maturity and gain the ability to reproduce?

At what age does reproduction stop?

Do they mate with only one partner or have multiple partners?

How are mates chosen?

Which genders can reproduce and how is it done?

How often do they reproduce and how many children are born at a time?

How long does pregnancy last?

What are the physical, emotional, and social effects of pregnancy on an individual?

Major Race 1: Reproduction

What are the social effects of pregnancy on the pregnant individual's partner(s) and their families?

_____

_____

_____

What methods are used to prevent pregnancy?

_____

_____

What methods are used to encourage pregnancy?

_____

_____

What methods are used to terminate a pregnancy?

_____

_____

What are the social effects of a terminated pregnancy?

_____

_____

Describe the birthing process. Who assist with the process?

_____

_____

_____

_____

What are common risks associated with birth?

_____

_____

What other races can they reproduce with?

What is the result of a child conceived by a member of this race and another race?

What differences occur in a pregnancy of a child conceived between a member of this race and another race?

What differences occur in the birth of a child conceived between a member of this race and another race?

What role does government and religion have in reproduction?

What role does magic and technology have in reproduction?

What is the social effect of reproduction occurring outside of marriage?

Special Occasions

List a few special occasions they observe.

1.	8.
2.	9.
3.	10.
4.	11.
5.	12.
6.	13.
7.	14.

Describe a few special occasions they observe.

Name: Date:

Notes:

Name: Date:

Notes:

Name: Date:

Notes:

Name: Date:

Notes:

Leisure Activities

What leisure activities are enjoyed by children?

_____

_____

_____

What leisure activities are enjoyed by adolescents?

_____

_____

_____

What leisure activities are enjoyed by adults?

_____

_____

_____

What leisure activities are enjoyed by the elderly?

_____

_____

_____

Describe leisure sports that are played and who can participate.

_____

_____

_____

Describe competitive sports that are played and who can participate.

_____

_____

_____

Major Race 1: Leisure Activities

Describe a few notable athletic competitions.

Name: Date:

Notes:

Name: Date:

Notes:

Name: Date:

Notes:

Describe a few notable athletes.

Name: Period Lived:

Notes:

Name: Period Lived:

Notes:

Name: Period Lived:

Notes:

Pets

What creatures are kept as pets?

_____

_____

_____

Who can own pets?

_____

_____

What services are provided by pets?

_____

_____

_____

Where are pets kept?

_____

_____

_____

Where are pets acquired from?

_____

How are pets trained?

_____

_____

How are pets and pet owners treated in society?

_____

_____

_____

Art

How important is art in their society?

_____

What art exists and what are their subjects?

_____

_____

_____

Where did their art originate?

_____

What materials are used to create their art?

_____

_____

_____

What influence has art had on their society?

_____

_____

_____

What special groups of artists exist?

_____

_____

_____

How are artists treated in society?

_____

_____

_____

Describe a few notable pieces of art.

Name: _____ Subject: _____

Notes: _____

_____

_____

Name: _____ Subject: _____

Notes: _____

_____

_____

Name: _____ Subject: _____

Notes: _____

_____

_____

Describe a few notable artists.

Name: _____ Period Lived: _____

Notes: _____

_____

_____

Name: _____ Period Lived: _____

Notes: _____

_____

_____

Name: _____ Period Lived: _____

Notes: _____

_____

_____

Architecture

What materials are used to create their buildings?

_____

_____

_____

Describe their architectural style.

_____

_____

_____

Describe a few common buildings.

Name: Use:
Notes:
_____

_____

_____

Name: Use:
Notes:
_____

_____

_____

Name: Use:
Notes:
_____

_____

_____

Name: Use:
Notes:
_____

_____

_____

Describe a few notable buildings.

Name: Location:

Notes:

Name: Location:

Notes:

Name: Location:

Notes:

Describe a few notable architects.

Name: Period Lived:

Notes:

Name: Period Lived:

Notes:

Name: Period Lived:

Notes:

Literature

How common is their ability to read?

How important is literature in their society?

What written records exist and what are their subjects?

What materials are used to record their literature?

What influence has literature had on their society?

What special groups of writers exist?

How are writers treated in society?

Describe a few notable pieces of literature.

Name: _____ Subject: _____

Notes: _____

_____

_____

Name: _____ Subject: _____

Notes: _____

_____

_____

Name: _____ Subject: _____

Notes: _____

_____

_____

Describe a few notable authors.

Name: _____ Period Lived: _____

Notes: _____

_____

_____

Name: _____ Period Lived: _____

Notes: _____

_____

_____

Name: _____ Period Lived: _____

Notes: _____

_____

_____

Music

How important is music in their society?

_____

What kinds of music exist and what purpose does music serve?

_____

_____

_____

Where did their music originate?

_____

What instruments are used to create their music?

_____

_____

_____

What influence has music had on their society?

_____

_____

_____

What special groups of musicians exist?

_____

_____

_____

How are musicians treated in society?

_____

_____

_____

Describe a few notable pieces of music.

Name: _____ Subject: _____

Notes: _____

_____

_____

Name: _____ Subject: _____

Notes: _____

_____

_____

Name: _____ Subject: _____

Notes: _____

_____

_____

Describe a few notable musicians.

Name: _____ Period Lived: _____

Notes: _____

_____

_____

Name: _____ Period Lived: _____

Notes: _____

_____

_____

Name: _____ Period Lived: _____

Notes: _____

_____

_____

Dance

How important is dance in their society?

_____

What kinds of dances exist and what purpose does dancing serve?

_____

_____

_____

Where did their dance originate?

_____

What outfits, accessories, and props are used during their dances?

_____

_____

_____

What influence has dance had on their society?

_____

_____

_____

What special groups of dancers exist?

_____

_____

_____

How are dancers treated in society?

_____

_____

_____

Describe a few notable dances.

Name: Subject:
_____

Notes:
_____

_____

_____

Name: Subject:
_____

Notes:
_____

_____

_____

Name: Subject:
_____

Notes:
_____

_____

_____

Describe a few notable dancers.

Name: Period Lived:
_____

Notes:
_____

_____

_____

Name: Period Lived:
_____

Notes:
_____

_____

_____

Name: Period Lived:
_____

Notes:
_____

_____

_____

Philosophy

How important is philosophy in their society?

What philosophies exist and what are their subjects?

Where did their philosophies originate?

What methods are used to communicate philosophies?

What influence has philosophy had on their society?

What special groups of philosophers exist?

How are philosophers treated in society?

Describe a few notable philosophies.

Name: Subject:

Notes:

Name: Subject:

Notes:

Name: Subject:

Notes:

Describe a few notable philosophers.

Name: Period Lived:

Notes:

Name: Period Lived:

Notes:

Name: Period Lived:

Notes:

Notes on Major Race 1: _____

Notes on Major Race 1: _____

Major Race 2: _____

Basics

What do they call themselves and what do others call them?

_____

_____

_____

Describe them in three words.

_____   _____   _____

What is the most well-known fact or accepted belief about them?

_____

_____

_____

What is their most guarded secret?

_____

_____

_____

What is the most important part of their society?

_____

_____

_____

Where does most of their population live?

_____

_____

Characteristics

Describe their average physical form.

_____

_____

_____

_____

_____

Draw or paste an image of their average physical form.

Major Race 2: Characteristics

Describe their ideal physical form.

_____

_____

_____

Describe their magical and technological characteristics.

_____

_____

_____

_____

Describe their physical characteristics.

_____

_____

_____

Describe their social characteristics.

_____

_____

_____

Describe their skills and abilities.

_____

_____

_____

Describe their attitude towards other races.

_____

_____

_____

Social Hierarchy

Describe their social hierarchy.

_____

_____

_____

Draw their social hierarchy.

How does an individual's or family's social status affect their daily life?

_____

_____

_____

How can an individual's or family's social status change?

_____

_____

_____

Gender Differences

Describe their genders.

_____

_____

_____

What are the physical differences between genders?

_____

_____

_____

What are the cognitive differences between genders?

_____

_____

_____

What are the perceived and societal gender differences for children?

_____

_____

_____

What are the perceived and societal gender differences for adults?

_____

_____

_____

How do members of different genders commonly interact?

_____

_____

_____

Language

What is the name of the language they speak or sign?

_____

Is the language also written?

_____

Describe how their language sounds and its basic principles.

_____

_____

_____

How and where did their language originate?

_____

_____

_____

How do they communicate with each other?

_____

_____

_____

How do they communicate with other races?

_____

_____

_____

How do they send messages near and far?

_____

_____

_____

Major Race 2: Language

Describe a few common words of their language.

Spoken / Signed Word	Written Word	Translation

Describe a few common phrases of their language.

Spoken / Signed Phrase	Written Phrase	Translation

Names

How are names chosen?

_____

_____

_____

How are names changed?

_____

_____

_____

What significance does a name have on an individual?

_____

_____

_____

How many parts are in a name?

_____

List a few first, female, or other gendered names.

1. _____   5. _____
2. _____   6. _____
3. _____   7. _____
4. _____   8. _____

List a few middle, male, or other gendered names.

1. _____   5. _____
2. _____   6. _____
3. _____   7. _____
4. _____   8. _____

Major Race 2: Names

List a few last, family, or identifying names.

1. _____   6. _____

2. _____   7. _____

3. _____   8. _____

4. _____   9. _____

5. _____   10. _____

List a few titles they can acquire.

Title	Acquired By
1.	
2.	
3.	
4.	
5.	
6.	
7.	
8.	
9.	
10.	
11.	
12.	

Describe how titles may be changed.

_____

_____

_____

Describe the social impact of titles.

_____

_____

_____

Religion

How important is religion in their society? Which religion dominates their culture?

_____

_____

_____

What purpose does religion serve in their society?

_____

_____

_____

What are their beliefs about the beginning of life?

_____

_____

_____

What are their beliefs about death, afterlife, and reincarnation?

_____

_____

_____

Where are how do they practice their religion?

_____

_____

_____

How tolerant of other religious beliefs are they?

_____

_____

_____

Major Race 2: Religion

Describe a few of their deities or important religious individuals.

Name:

Notes:

Name:

Notes:

Name:

Notes:

Name:

Notes:

Name:

Notes:

Name:

Notes:

Describe a few important religious teachings they follow or rituals they perform.

Name:

Notes:

Name:

Notes:

Name:

Notes:

Name:

Notes:

Name:

Notes:

Name:

Notes:

Magic

How important is magic in their society?

_____

What influence has magic had on their society?

_____

_____

_____

What purpose does magic serve in their society?

_____

_____

_____

What do they call their magicians and what do their magicians call themselves?

_____

_____

_____

Describe how they use magic.

_____

_____

_____

Where did their magical knowledge originate?

_____

Who can become a magician?

_____

_____

_____

How are magicians educated?

How are magicians treated in society?

What laws, governing or religious, pertain specifically to magicians?

How do magicians commonly interact with each other?

What special groups of magicians exist?

Describe the hierarchy of magicians.

Major Race 2: Magic

Describe a few notable magicians or spells.

Name:

Notes:

Name:

Notes:

Name:

Notes:

Name:

Notes:

Name:

Notes:

Name:

Notes:

Technology

How important is technology in their society?

_____

What influence has technology had on their society?

_____

_____

_____

What purpose does technology serve in their society?

_____

_____

_____

What do they call their technology, and what do others call it?

_____

_____

_____

Describe how they use technology.

_____

_____

_____

How much of their technology is borrowed or copied from other races?

_____

Who can become an inventor and technology user?

_____

_____

_____

Major Race 2: Technology

How are inventors and technology users educated?

_____

_____

_____

How are inventors and technology users treated in society?

_____

_____

_____

What laws, governing or religious, pertain specifically to technology users?

_____

_____

_____

How do inventors and technology users commonly interact with each other?

_____

_____

_____

What special groups of inventors and technology users exist?

_____

_____

_____

Describe the hierarchy of inventors and technology users.

_____

_____

_____

Describe a few notable inventors or inventions.

Name:

Notes:

Name:

Notes:

Name:

Notes:

Name:

Notes:

Name:

Notes:

Name:

Notes:

Government

Describe their government.

_____

_____

_____

Who can be a government official?

_____

_____

_____

Who can participate in the government?

_____

_____

_____

What influence does government have in their society?

_____

_____

_____

Describe a few impactful events in the history of their government.

Name: Date:

Notes:

_____

_____

_____

Name: Date:

Notes:

_____

_____

List a few notable laws of their government.

Name: Date Enacted:

Notes:

Name: Date Enacted:

Notes:

Name: Date Enacted:

Notes:

Name: Date Enacted:

Notes:

Name: Date Enacted:

Notes:

Name: Date Enacted:

Notes:

Major Race 2: Government

Describe their foreign policies.

_____

_____

_____

Describe their treaties and alliances.

_____

_____

_____

Describe their rivals and enemies.

_____

_____

_____

Describe a few notable members of their government.

Name: Period Lived:
_____
Notes:
_____

_____

Name: Period Lived:
_____
Notes:
_____

_____

Name: Period Lived:
_____
Notes:
_____

_____

War

Describe their attitude towards war and physical conflicts.

_____

_____

_____

Describe how their society has been affected by war.

_____

_____

_____

Describe a few wars from their history.

Name: Time Period:
_____
Notes:
_____

_____

Name: Time Period:
_____
Notes:
_____

_____

Name: Time Period:
_____
Notes:
_____

_____

Name: Time Period:
_____
Notes:
_____

_____

Major Race 2: War

Describe a few of their weapons and armor.

Name: Material:

Notes:
_____

_____

Name: Material:

Notes:
_____

_____

Name: Material:

Notes:
_____

_____

Describe a few famous warriors and peacekeepers.

Name: Period Lived:

Notes:
_____

_____

Name: Period Lived:

Notes:
_____

_____

Name: Period Lived:

Notes:
_____

_____

History

How and where did they originate from?

_____

_____

_____

Briefly describe their history.

_____

_____

_____

Describe a few important events in their history.

Name: Date:

Notes:

_____

_____

Name: Date:

Notes:

_____

_____

Name: Date:

Notes:

_____

_____

Name: Date:

Notes:

_____

_____

Achievements

What do they consider their greatest achievement?

_____

_____

_____

What effect have their achievements had on the world?

_____

_____

_____

Describe a few additional achievements they have made.

Name: _____ Date: _____

Notes: _____

_____

_____

Name: _____ Date: _____

Notes: _____

_____

_____

Name: _____ Date: _____

Notes: _____

_____

_____

Name: _____ Date: _____

Notes: _____

_____

_____

Economics

What kind of currency is used?

_____

What is their currency made of and what does it look like?

_____

Who monitors and distributes their currency?

_____

_____

_____

What kind of trades can be made?

_____

_____

_____

How is their currency accepted by other races?

_____

_____

_____

Describe a few common valuations.

Item or Service	Trade or Monetary Value
1.	
2.	
3.	
4.	
5.	
6.	
7.	

Ownership System

What property can be owned?

_____

_____

_____

Who can own property?

_____

_____

_____

What laws and punishments exist regarding stolen and vandalized property?

_____

_____

_____

What happens to property when the owner dies?

_____

_____

_____

Describe slavery within your race and its impact on your world.

_____

_____

_____

_____

_____

_____

_____

_____

Cities

How many cities have they founded?

_____

Where and how were most cities founded?

_____

_____

_____

Describe a few notable cities.

Name: Location:
_____
Notes:
_____

_____

_____

Name: Location:
_____
Notes:
_____

_____

_____

Name: Location:
_____
Notes:
_____

_____

_____

Name: Location:
_____
Notes:
_____

_____

_____

Housing

In what type of building or area do they live? What is it made of?

_____

_____

_____

Describe how their homes are uniquely adapted to them.

_____

_____

_____

Describe their housing arrangements. Who lives together?

_____

_____

_____

Draw or paste a layout of a common home.

What special housing exists?

_____

_____

_____

Describe how wealth affects housing.

_____

_____

_____

Describe the furniture and items found in their homes.

_____

_____

_____

Draw or paste a layout of a special or wealthy home.

Education

Describe their educational system.

_____

_____

_____

List a few subjects that are taught.

1.	9.
2.	10.
3.	11.
4.	12.
5.	13.
6.	14.
7.	15.
8.	16.

Who are the instructors?

_____

_____

_____

Describe their special schools and educational programs.

_____

_____

_____

Who can attend school and who can obtain special education?

_____

_____

_____

Describe a few notable schools.

Name: Location:
_____

Notes:
_____

_____

_____

Name: Location:
_____

Notes:
_____

_____

_____

Name: Location:
_____

Notes:
_____

_____

_____

Describe a few notable educators.

Name: Period Lived:
_____

Notes:
_____

_____

_____

Name: Period Lived:
_____

Notes:
_____

_____

_____

Name: Period Lived:
_____

Notes:
_____

_____

_____

Professions

List a few common professions.

1. _____   5. _____

2. _____   6. _____

3. _____   7. _____

4. _____   8. _____

List a few necessary but uncommon professions.

1. _____   3. _____

2. _____   4. _____

How are professions chosen?

_____

_____

_____

How are professions able to be changed?

_____

_____

_____

How does an individual acquire their professional education?

_____

_____

_____

Describe a few professions and their trade or monetary earnings.

	Profession	Trade or Monetary Value
1.		
2.		
3.		

Health

What is the name of their medical practitioners?

_____

Who can be a medical practitioner?

_____

How are medical practitioners educated?

_____

_____

_____

What treatments or medicines are used?

_____

_____

_____

What medical instruments are used?

_____

_____

_____

Does their medicine work on other races?

_____

Describe a few diseases, infections, or sicknesses they can be affected with.

_____

_____

_____

Diet

What does their diet primarily consist of?

_____

_____

How much and how often do they eat?

_____

What utensils are used to prepare and cook food?

_____

_____

What methods is food prepared?

_____

_____

What food sources are gathered?

_____

_____

What food sources are grown or raised?

_____

_____

What food sources are hunted?

_____

_____

What food sources are traded?

_____

_____

Daily Life

Where do they eat?

_____

When are common mealtimes?

_____

Where do they sleep?

_____

When do they sleep and for how long?

_____

What and how do they breathe?

_____

_____

Where and how do they release waste?

_____

_____

Describe their mealtime practices.

_____

_____

_____

Describe their travel arrangements.

_____

_____

_____

Clothing

What are their clothes made of?

What do children wear?

What do adults wear?

What effect does gender have on their clothing?

What accessories do they wear?

What piercings, tattoos or other optional markings can they have?

Describe a few outfits.

Worn By or For:	
Notes:	

Worn By or For:	
Notes:	

Worn By or For:	
Notes:	

Worn By or For:	
Notes:	

Grooming

How do they groom themselves? How often is it done?

_____

_____

_____

Where do they groom themselves?

_____

_____

_____

How do they view their grooming habits?

_____

_____

_____

How do other races view their grooming habits?

_____

_____

_____

What items are used and what habits are common for female grooming?

_____

_____

_____

What items are used and what habits are common for male grooming?

_____

_____

_____

Children

How are children treated in society?

_____

_____

_____

Who do children reside with?

_____

How are children educated?

_____

_____

_____

Where and with whom do children spend most of their time?

_____

_____

_____

What are a few special events in a child's life?

_____

_____

_____

At what age are children considered to be adolescents?

_____

Describe the experience of becoming an adolescent.

_____

_____

_____

Adolescents

How are adolescents treated in society?

_____

_____

_____

Where and with whom do adolescents spend most of their time?

_____

How are adolescents educated?

_____

_____

What are a few special events in an adolescent's life?

_____

_____

_____

At what age are adolescents considered to be adults?

_____

Describe the physical changes associated with becoming an adult.

_____

_____

_____

Describe the social changes associated with becoming an adult.

_____

_____

Adults

How are adults treated in society?

Where and with whom do adults spend most of their time?

How are adults educated?

What are a few special events in an adult's life?

At what age are adults considered to be elderly?

Describe the physical changes associated with becoming elderly.

Describe the social changes associated with becoming elderly.

The Elderly

How are the elderly treated in society?

_____

_____

_____

What special treatments exist to honor the elderly?

_____

_____

Where and with whom do the elderly spend most of their time?

_____

_____

_____

What are a few special events in an elder's life?

_____

_____

_____

At what age do the elderly die?

_____

What ways exist to reverse the aging process or prolong the life of the elderly?

_____

_____

What influence do they elderly have on society?

_____

_____

_____

Etiquette

What is the proper relationship between the young and the elderly?

_____

_____

_____

What is the proper relationship between child and parent?

_____

_____

_____

What is the proper relationship between siblings?

_____

_____

_____

Describe a few examples of proper etiquette.

Situation:
_____

Acceptable Etiquette:
_____

Situation:
_____

Acceptable Etiquette:
_____

Situation:
_____

Acceptable Etiquette:
_____

Death

What ritual is performed after death?

_____

_____

_____

Who participates in the ritual?

_____

_____

_____

What happens to the corpse of the dead?

_____

_____

_____

In what ways are the dead honored or remembered?

_____

_____

_____

How does death affect society and an individual's family?

_____

_____

_____

List the most common causes of death.

1. _____	5. _____
2. _____	6. _____
3. _____	7. _____
4. _____	8. _____

Courtship & Marriage

How are potential partners selected for courtship?

_____

_____

How is courtship initiated?

_____

_____

Describe the process of courtship.

_____

_____

_____

What is it called to be married?

_____

Under what governing law or ceremony can individuals marry and is it for life?

_____

_____

Describe the events that come before the ceremony and interactions between the individuals.

_____

_____

_____

Describe the marriage ceremony.

_____

_____

_____

Major Race 2: Courtship & Marriage

What are the social effects of marriage on the individuals?

_____

_____

_____

What are the social effects of marriage on the individuals' families?

_____

_____

_____

Describe the religious or government laws of marriage.

_____

_____

_____

Under what circumstances can the religious or governmental marriage laws be broken?

_____

_____

_____

What are the social effects on individuals if the religious or governmental marriage law is broken?

_____

_____

_____

If a married individual dies can the surviving partner(s) participate in a new marriage ceremony?

_____

_____

_____

Reproduction

At what age do they reach sexual maturity and gain the ability to reproduce?

_____

At what age does reproduction stop?

_____

Do they mate with only one partner or have multiple partners?

_____

How are mates chosen?

_____

_____

Which genders can reproduce and how is it done?

_____

_____

_____

How often do they reproduce and how many children are born at a time?

_____

How long does pregnancy last?

_____

What are the physical, emotional, and social effects of pregnancy on an individual?

_____

_____

_____

_____

_____

Major Race 2: Reproduction

What are the social effects of pregnancy on the pregnant individual's partner(s) and their families?

_____

_____

_____

What methods are used to prevent pregnancy?

_____

_____

What methods are used to encourage pregnancy?

_____

_____

What methods are used to terminate a pregnancy?

_____

_____

What are the social effects of a terminated pregnancy?

_____

_____

Describe the birthing process. Who assist with the process?

_____

_____

_____

_____

What are common risks associated with birth?

_____

_____

What other races can they reproduce with?

_____

What is the result of a child conceived by a member of this race and another race?

_____

_____

_____

What differences occur in a pregnancy of a child conceived between a member of this race and another race?

_____

_____

What differences occur in the birth of a child conceived between a member of this race and another race?

_____

_____

What role does government and religion have in reproduction?

_____

_____

_____

What role does magic and technology have in reproduction?

_____

_____

_____

What is the social effect of reproduction occurring outside of marriage?

_____

_____

Special Occasions

List a few special occasions they observe.

1. _____   8. _____

2. _____   9. _____

3. _____   10. _____

4. _____   11. _____

5. _____   12. _____

6. _____   13. _____

7. _____   14. _____

Describe a few special occasions they observe.

Name: _____   Date: _____

Notes: _____

_____

_____

Name: _____   Date: _____

Notes: _____

_____

_____

Name: _____   Date: _____

Notes: _____

_____

_____

Name: _____   Date: _____

Notes: _____

_____

_____

Leisure Activities

What leisure activities are enjoyed by children?

_____

_____

_____

What leisure activities are enjoyed by adolescents?

_____

_____

_____

What leisure activities are enjoyed by adults?

_____

_____

_____

What leisure activities are enjoyed by the elderly?

_____

_____

_____

Describe leisure sports that are played and who can participate.

_____

_____

_____

Describe competitive sports that are played and who can participate.

_____

_____

_____

Major Race 2: Leisure Activities

Describe a few notable athletic competitions.

Name: Date:

Notes:

_____

_____

Name: Date:

Notes:

_____

_____

Name: Date:

Notes:

_____

_____

Describe a few notable athletes.

Name: Period Lived:

Notes:

_____

_____

Name: Period Lived:

Notes:

_____

_____

Name: Period Lived:

Notes:

_____

_____

Pets

What creatures are kept as pets?

_____

_____

_____

Who can own pets?

_____

_____

What services are provided by pets?

_____

_____

_____

Where are pets kept?

_____

_____

_____

Where are pets acquired from?

_____

How are pets trained?

_____

_____

How are pets and pet owners treated in society?

_____

_____

_____

Art

How important is art in their society?

_____

What art exists and what are their subjects?

_____

_____

_____

Where did their art originate?

_____

What materials are used to create their art?

_____

_____

_____

What influence has art had on their society?

_____

_____

_____

What special groups of artists exist?

_____

_____

_____

How are artists treated in society?

_____

_____

_____

Describe a few notable pieces of art.

Name: _____ Subject: _____

Notes: _____

_____

_____

Name: _____ Subject: _____

Notes: _____

_____

_____

Name: _____ Subject: _____

Notes: _____

_____

_____

Describe a few notable artists.

Name: _____ Period Lived: _____

Notes: _____

_____

_____

Name: _____ Period Lived: _____

Notes: _____

_____

_____

Name: _____ Period Lived: _____

Notes: _____

_____

_____

Architecture

What materials are used to create their buildings?

_____

_____

_____

Describe their architectural style.

_____

_____

_____

Describe a few common buildings.

Name: Use:
_____

Notes:
_____

_____

Name: Use:
_____

Notes:
_____

_____

Name: Use:
_____

Notes:
_____

_____

Name: Use:
_____

Notes:
_____

_____

Describe a few notable buildings.

Name: _____ Location: _____

Notes: _____

_____

_____

Name: _____ Location: _____

Notes: _____

_____

_____

Name: _____ Location: _____

Notes: _____

_____

_____

Describe a few notable architects.

Name: _____ Period Lived: _____

Notes: _____

_____

_____

Name: _____ Period Lived: _____

Notes: _____

_____

_____

Name: _____ Period Lived: _____

Notes: _____

_____

_____

Literature

How common is their ability to read?

_____

How important is literature in their society?

_____

What written records exist and what are their subjects?

_____

_____

_____

What materials are used to record their literature?

_____

_____

_____

What influence has literature had on their society?

_____

_____

_____

What special groups of writers exist?

_____

_____

_____

How are writers treated in society?

_____

_____

_____

Describe a few notable pieces of literature.

Name: Subject:

Notes:

Name: Subject:

Notes:

Name: Subject:

Notes:

Describe a few notable authors.

Name: Period Lived:

Notes:

Name: Period Lived:

Notes:

Name: Period Lived:

Notes:

Music

How important is music in their society?

_____

What kinds of music exist and what purpose does music serve?

_____

_____

_____

Where did their music originate?

_____

What instruments are used to create their music?

_____

_____

_____

What influence has music had on their society?

_____

_____

_____

What special groups of musicians exist?

_____

_____

_____

How are musicians treated in society?

_____

_____

_____

Describe a few notable pieces of music.

Name: Subject:

Notes:

Name: Subject:

Notes:

Name: Subject:

Notes:

Describe a few notable musicians.

Name: Period Lived:

Notes:

Name: Period Lived:

Notes:

Name: Period Lived:

Notes:

Dance

How important is dance in their society?

_____

What kinds of dances exist and what purpose does dancing serve?

_____

_____

_____

Where did their dance originate?

_____

What outfits, accessories, and props are used during their dances?

_____

_____

_____

What influence has dance had on their society?

_____

_____

_____

What special groups of dancers exist?

_____

_____

_____

How are dancers treated in society?

_____

_____

_____

Describe a few notable dances.

Name: _____ Subject: _____

Notes: _____

_____

_____

Name: _____ Subject: _____

Notes: _____

_____

_____

Name: _____ Subject: _____

Notes: _____

_____

_____

Describe a few notable dancers.

Name: _____ Period Lived: _____

Notes: _____

_____

_____

Name: _____ Period Lived: _____

Notes: _____

_____

_____

Name: _____ Period Lived: _____

Notes: _____

_____

_____

Philosophy

How important is philosophy in their society?

_____

What philosophies exist and what are their subjects?

_____

_____

_____

Where did their philosophies originate?

_____

What methods are used to communicate philosophies?

_____

_____

_____

What influence has philosophy had on their society?

_____

_____

_____

What special groups of philosophers exist?

_____

_____

_____

How are philosophers treated in society?

_____

_____

_____

Describe a few notable philosophies.

Name: _____ Subject: _____

Notes: _____

_____

_____

Name: _____ Subject: _____

Notes: _____

_____

_____

Name: _____ Subject: _____

Notes: _____

_____

_____

Describe a few notable philosophers.

Name: _____ Period Lived: _____

Notes: _____

_____

_____

Name: _____ Period Lived: _____

Notes: _____

_____

_____

Name: _____ Period Lived: _____

Notes: _____

_____

_____

Notes on Major Race 2: _____

Notes on Major Race 2: _____

Major Race 3: _____

Basics

What do they call themselves and what do others call them?

_____

_____

_____

Describe them in three words.

_____ _____ _____

What is the most well-known fact or accepted belief about them?

_____

_____

_____

What is their most guarded secret?

_____

_____

_____

What is the most important part of their society?

_____

_____

_____

Where does most of their population live?

_____

_____

Characteristics

Describe their average physical form.

_____

_____

_____

_____

_____

Draw or paste an image of their average physical form.

Major Race 3: Characteristics

Describe their ideal physical form.

_____

_____

_____

Describe their magical and technological characteristics.

_____

_____

_____

_____

Describe their physical characteristics.

_____

_____

_____

Describe their social characteristics.

_____

_____

_____

Describe their skills and abilities.

_____

_____

_____

Describe their attitude towards other races.

_____

_____

_____

Social Hierarchy

Describe their social hierarchy.

_____

_____

_____

Draw their social hierarchy.

How does an individual's or family's social status affect their daily life?

_____

_____

_____

How can an individual's or family's social status change?

_____

_____

_____

Gender Differences

Describe their genders.

_____

_____

_____

What are the physical differences between genders?

_____

_____

_____

What are the cognitive differences between genders?

_____

_____

_____

What are the perceived and societal gender differences for children?

_____

_____

_____

What are the perceived and societal gender differences for adults?

_____

_____

_____

How do members of different genders commonly interact?

_____

_____

_____

Language

What is the name of the language they speak or sign?

_____

Is the language also written?

_____

Describe how their language sounds and its basic principles.

_____

_____

_____

How and where did their language originate?

_____

_____

_____

How do they communicate with each other?

_____

_____

_____

How do they communicate with other races?

_____

_____

_____

How do they send messages near and far?

_____

_____

_____

Major Race 3: Language

Describe a few common words of their language.

Spoken / Signed Word	Written Word	Translation

Describe a few common phrases of their language.

Spoken / Signed Phrase	Written Phrase	Translation

Names

How are names chosen?

_____

_____

_____

How are names changed?

_____

_____

_____

What significance does a name have on an individual?

_____

_____

_____

How many parts are in a name?

_____

List a few first, female, or other gendered names.

1. _____   5. _____

2. _____   6. _____

3. _____   7. _____

4. _____   8. _____

List a few middle, male, or other gendered names.

1. _____   5. _____

2. _____   6. _____

3. _____   7. _____

4. _____   8. _____

Major Race 3: Names

List a few last, family, or identifying names.

1.	6.
2.	7.
3.	8.
4.	9.
5.	10.

List a few titles they can acquire.

Title	Acquired By
1.	
2.	
3.	
4.	
5.	
6.	
7.	
8.	
9.	
10.	
11.	
12.	

Describe how titles may be changed.

_____

_____

_____

Describe the social impact of titles.

_____

_____

_____

Religion

How important is religion in their society? Which religion dominates their culture?

_____

_____

_____

What purpose does religion serve in their society?

_____

_____

_____

What are their beliefs about the beginning of life?

_____

_____

_____

What are their beliefs about death, afterlife, and reincarnation?

_____

_____

_____

Where are how do they practice their religion?

_____

_____

_____

How tolerant of other religious beliefs are they?

_____

_____

_____

Major Race 3: Religion

Describe a few of their deities or important religious individuals.

Name:

Notes:

Name:

Notes:

Name:

Notes:

Name:

Notes:

Name:

Notes:

Name:

Notes:

Describe a few important religious teachings they follow or rituals they perform.

Name:

Notes:

Name:

Notes:

Name:

Notes:

Name:

Notes:

Name:

Notes:

Name:

Notes:

Major Race 3: Magic

Magic

How important is magic in their society?

_____

What influence has magic had on their society?

_____

_____

What purpose does magic serve in their society?

_____

_____

What do they call their magicians and what do their magicians call themselves?

_____

_____

Describe how they use magic.

_____

_____

Where did their magical knowledge originate?

_____

Who can become a magician?

_____

_____

How are magicians educated?

_____

_____

_____

How are magicians treated in society?

_____

_____

_____

What laws, governing or religious, pertain specifically to magicians?

_____

_____

_____

How do magicians commonly interact with each other?

_____

_____

_____

What special groups of magicians exist?

_____

_____

_____

Describe the hierarchy of magicians.

_____

_____

_____

Major Race 3: Magic

Describe a few notable magicians or spells.

Name:

Notes:

Name:

Notes:

Name:

Notes:

Name:

Notes:

Name:

Notes:

Name:

Notes:

Major Race 3: Magic

Technology

How important is technology in their society?

_____

What influence has technology had on their society?

_____

_____

_____

What purpose does technology serve in their society?

_____

_____

_____

What do they call their technology, and what do others call it?

_____

_____

_____

Describe how they use technology.

_____

_____

_____

How much of their technology is borrowed or copied from other races?

_____

Who can become an inventor and technology user?

_____

_____

_____

Major Race 3: Technology

How are inventors and technology users educated?

_____

_____

_____

How are inventors and technology users treated in society?

_____

_____

_____

What laws, governing or religious, pertain specifically to technology users?

_____

_____

_____

How do inventors and technology users commonly interact with each other?

_____

_____

_____

What special groups of inventors and technology users exist?

_____

_____

_____

Describe the hierarchy of inventors and technology users.

_____

_____

_____

Describe a few notable inventors or inventions.

Name:

Notes:

Name:

Notes:

Name:

Notes:

Name:

Notes:

Name:

Notes:

Name:

Notes:

Government

Describe their government.

_____

_____

_____

Who can be a government official?

_____

_____

_____

Who can participate in the government?

_____

_____

_____

What influence does government have in their society?

_____

_____

_____

Describe a few impactful events in the history of their government.

Name: Date:

Notes:

_____

_____

_____

Name: Date:

Notes:

_____

_____

_____

List a few notable laws of their government.

Name: _____ Date Enacted: _____

Notes: _____

_____

_____

Name: _____ Date Enacted: _____

Notes: _____

_____

_____

Name: _____ Date Enacted: _____

Notes: _____

_____

_____

Name: _____ Date Enacted: _____

Notes: _____

_____

_____

Name: _____ Date Enacted: _____

Notes: _____

_____

_____

Name: _____ Date Enacted: _____

Notes: _____

_____

_____

Major Race 3: Government

Describe their foreign policies.

_____

_____

_____

Describe their treaties and alliances.

_____

_____

_____

Describe their rivals and enemies.

_____

_____

_____

Describe a few notable members of their government.

Name: Period Lived:

Notes: _____

_____

_____

Name: Period Lived:

Notes: _____

_____

_____

Name: Period Lived:

Notes: _____

_____

_____

War

Describe their attitude towards war and physical conflicts.

_____

_____

_____

Describe how their society has been affected by war.

_____

_____

_____

Describe a few wars from their history.

Name: _____ Time Period: _____

Notes: _____

_____

Name: _____ Time Period: _____

Notes: _____

_____

Name: _____ Time Period: _____

Notes: _____

_____

Name: _____ Time Period: _____

Notes: _____

_____

Major Race 3: War

Describe a few of their weapons and armor.

Name: Material:
_____
Notes:
_____
_____

_____

Name: Material:
_____
Notes:
_____
_____

_____

Name: Material:
_____
Notes:
_____
_____

_____

Describe a few famous warriors and peacekeepers.

Name: Period Lived:
_____
Notes:
_____
_____

_____

Name: Period Lived:
_____
Notes:
_____
_____

_____

Name: Period Lived:
_____
Notes:
_____
_____

_____

History

How and where did they originate from?

_____

_____

_____

Briefly describe their history.

_____

_____

_____

Describe a few important events in their history.

Name: Date:

Notes:

_____

_____

Name: Date:

Notes:

_____

_____

Name: Date:

Notes:

_____

_____

Name: Date:

Notes:

_____

_____

Achievements

What do they consider their greatest achievement?

_____

_____

_____

What effect have their achievements had on the world?

_____

_____

_____

Describe a few additional achievements they have made.

Name: Date:
_____
Notes:
_____

_____

Name: Date:
_____
Notes:
_____

_____

Name: Date:
_____
Notes:
_____

_____

Name: Date:
_____
Notes:
_____

_____

Economics

What kind of currency is used?

_____

What is their currency made of and what does it look like?

_____

Who monitors and distributes their currency?

_____

_____

_____

What kind of trades can be made?

_____

_____

_____

How is their currency accepted by other races?

_____

_____

_____

Describe a few common valuations.

Item or Service	Trade or Monetary Value
1.	
2.	
3.	
4.	
5.	
6.	
7.	

Ownership System

What property can be owned?

_____

_____

_____

Who can own property?

_____

_____

_____

What laws and punishments exist regarding stolen and vandalized property?

_____

_____

_____

What happens to property when the owner dies?

_____

_____

_____

Describe slavery within your race and its impact on your world.

_____

_____

_____

_____

_____

_____

_____

_____

Cities

How many cities have they founded?

_____

Where and how were most cities founded?

_____

_____

_____

Describe a few notable cities.

Name: _____ Location: _____

Notes: _____

_____

_____

Name: _____ Location: _____

Notes: _____

_____

_____

Name: _____ Location: _____

Notes: _____

_____

_____

Name: _____ Location: _____

Notes: _____

_____

_____

Housing

In what type of building or area do they live? What is it made of?

_____

_____

_____

Describe how their homes are uniquely adapted to them.

_____

_____

_____

Describe their housing arrangements. Who lives together?

_____

_____

_____

Draw or paste a layout of a common home.

What special housing exists?

_____

_____

_____

Describe how wealth affects housing.

_____

_____

_____

Describe the furniture and items found in their homes.

_____

_____

_____

Draw or paste a layout of a special or wealthy home.

Major Race 3: Education

Education

Describe their educational system.

_____
_____
_____

List a few subjects that are taught.

1. _____   9. _____
2. _____   10. _____
3. _____   11. _____
4. _____   12. _____
5. _____   13. _____
6. _____   14. _____
7. _____   15. _____
8. _____   16. _____

Who are the instructors?

_____
_____
_____

Describe their special schools and educational programs.

_____
_____
_____

Who can attend school and who can obtain special education?

_____
_____
_____

Describe a few notable schools.

Name: _____ Location: _____

Notes: _____

_____

_____

Name: _____ Location: _____

Notes: _____

_____

_____

Name: _____ Location: _____

Notes: _____

_____

_____

Describe a few notable educators.

Name: _____ Period Lived: _____

Notes: _____

_____

_____

Name: _____ Period Lived: _____

Notes: _____

_____

_____

Name: _____ Period Lived: _____

Notes: _____

_____

_____

Professions

List a few common professions.

1. _____   5. _____

2. _____   6. _____

3. _____   7. _____

4. _____   8. _____

List a few necessary but uncommon professions.

1. _____   3. _____

2. _____   4. _____

How are professions chosen?

_____

_____

_____

How are professions able to be changed?

_____

_____

_____

How does an individual acquire their professional education?

_____

_____

_____

Describe a few professions and their trade or monetary earnings.

	Profession	Trade or Monetary Value
1.		
2.		
3.		

Health

What is the name of their medical practitioners?

_____

Who can be a medical practitioner?

_____

How are medical practitioners educated?

_____

_____

_____

What treatments or medicines are used?

_____

_____

_____

What medical instruments are used?

_____

_____

_____

Does their medicine work on other races?

_____

Describe a few diseases, infections, or sicknesses they can be affected with.

_____

_____

_____

Diet

What does their diet primarily consist of?

_____

_____

How much and how often do they eat?

_____

What utensils are used to prepare and cook food?

_____

_____

What methods is food prepared?

_____

_____

What food sources are gathered?

_____

_____

What food sources are grown or raised?

_____

_____

What food sources are hunted?

_____

_____

What food sources are traded?

_____

_____

Daily Life

Where do they eat?

_____

When are common mealtimes?

_____

Where do they sleep?

_____

When do they sleep and for how long?

_____

What and how do they breathe?

_____

_____

Where and how do they release waste?

_____

_____

Describe their mealtime practices.

_____

_____

_____

Describe their travel arrangements.

_____

_____

_____

Clothing

What are their clothes made of?

_____

_____

_____

What do children wear?

_____

_____

_____

What do adults wear?

_____

_____

_____

What effect does gender have on their clothing?

_____

_____

_____

What accessories do they wear?

_____

_____

_____

What piercings, tattoos or other optional markings can they have?

_____

_____

_____

Describe a few outfits.

Worn By or For:	
Notes:	

Worn By or For:	
Notes:	

Worn By or For:	
Notes:	

Worn By or For:	
Notes:	

Grooming

How do they groom themselves? How often is it done?

_____

_____

_____

Where do they groom themselves?

_____

_____

_____

How do they view their grooming habits?

_____

_____

_____

How do other races view their grooming habits?

_____

_____

_____

What items are used and what habits are common for female grooming?

_____

_____

_____

What items are used and what habits are common for male grooming?

_____

_____

_____

Children

How are children treated in society?

_____

_____

_____

Who do children reside with?

_____

How are children educated?

_____

_____

_____

Where and with whom do children spend most of their time?

_____

_____

_____

What are a few special events in a child's life?

_____

_____

_____

At what age are children considered to be adolescents?

_____

Describe the experience of becoming an adolescent.

_____

_____

_____

Adolescents

How are adolescents treated in society?

_____

_____

_____

Where and with whom do adolescents spend most of their time?

_____

How are adolescents educated?

_____

_____

What are a few special events in an adolescent's life?

_____

_____

_____

At what age are adolescents considered to be adults?

_____

Describe the physical changes associated with becoming an adult.

_____

_____

_____

Describe the social changes associated with becoming an adult.

_____

_____

_____

Adults

How are adults treated in society?

Where and with whom do adults spend most of their time?

How are adults educated?

What are a few special events in an adult's life?

At what age are adults considered to be elderly?

Describe the physical changes associated with becoming elderly.

Describe the social changes associated with becoming elderly.

The Elderly

How are the elderly treated in society?

_____

_____

_____

What special treatments exist to honor the elderly?

_____

_____

Where and with whom do the elderly spend most of their time?

_____

_____

_____

What are a few special events in an elder's life?

_____

_____

_____

At what age do the elderly die?

_____

What ways exist to reverse the aging process or prolong the life of the elderly?

_____

_____

What influence do they elderly have on society?

_____

_____

_____

Etiquette

What is the proper relationship between the young and the elderly?

_____

_____

_____

What is the proper relationship between child and parent?

_____

_____

_____

What is the proper relationship between siblings?

_____

_____

_____

Describe a few examples of proper etiquette.

Situation:
_____

Acceptable Etiquette:
_____

Situation:
_____

Acceptable Etiquette:
_____

Situation:
_____

Acceptable Etiquette:
_____

Death

What ritual is performed after death?

_____

_____

_____

Who participates in the ritual?

_____

_____

_____

What happens to the corpse of the dead?

_____

_____

_____

In what ways are the dead honored or remembered?

_____

_____

_____

How does death affect society and an individual's family?

_____

_____

_____

List the most common causes of death.

1. _____   5. _____

2. _____   6. _____

3. _____   7. _____

4. _____   8. _____

Courtship & Marriage

How are potential partners selected for courtship?

_____

_____

How is courtship initiated?

_____

_____

Describe the process of courtship.

_____

_____

_____

What is it called to be married?

_____

Under what governing law or ceremony can individuals marry and is it for life?

_____

_____

Describe the events that come before the ceremony and interactions between the individuals.

_____

_____

_____

Describe the marriage ceremony.

_____

_____

_____

Major Race 3: Courtship & Marriage

What are the social effects of marriage on the individuals?

_____

_____

_____

What are the social effects of marriage on the individuals' families?

_____

_____

_____

Describe the religious or government laws of marriage.

_____

_____

_____

Under what circumstances can the religious or governmental marriage laws be broken?

_____

_____

_____

What are the social effects on individuals if the religious or governmental marriage law is broken?

_____

_____

_____

If a married individual dies can the surviving partner(s) participate in a new marriage ceremony?

_____

_____

_____

Reproduction

At what age do they reach sexual maturity and gain the ability to reproduce?

At what age does reproduction stop?

Do they mate with only one partner or have multiple partners?

How are mates chosen?

Which genders can reproduce and how is it done?

How often do they reproduce and how many children are born at a time?

How long does pregnancy last?

What are the physical, emotional, and social effects of pregnancy on an individual?

Major Race 3: Reproduction

What are the social effects of pregnancy on the pregnant individual's partner(s) and their families?

_____

_____

_____

What methods are used to prevent pregnancy?

_____

_____

What methods are used to encourage pregnancy?

_____

_____

What methods are used to terminate a pregnancy?

_____

_____

What are the social effects of a terminated pregnancy?

_____

_____

Describe the birthing process. Who assist with the process?

_____

_____

_____

_____

What are common risks associated with birth?

_____

_____

What other races can they reproduce with?

_____

What is the result of a child conceived by a member of this race and another race?

_____

_____

_____

What differences occur in a pregnancy of a child conceived between a member of this race and another race?

_____

_____

What differences occur in the birth of a child conceived between a member of this race and another race?

_____

_____

What role does government and religion have in reproduction?

_____

_____

_____

What role does magic and technology have in reproduction?

_____

_____

_____

What is the social effect of reproduction occurring outside of marriage?

_____

_____

Special Occasions

List a few special occasions they observe.

1.	8.
2.	9.
3.	10.
4.	11.
5.	12.
6.	13.
7.	14.

Describe a few special occasions they observe.

Name: Date:

Notes:

Name: Date:

Notes:

Name: Date:

Notes:

Name: Date:

Notes:

Leisure Activities

What leisure activities are enjoyed by children?

_____

_____

_____

What leisure activities are enjoyed by adolescents?

_____

_____

_____

What leisure activities are enjoyed by adults?

_____

_____

_____

What leisure activities are enjoyed by the elderly?

_____

_____

_____

Describe leisure sports that are played and who can participate.

_____

_____

_____

Describe competitive sports that are played and who can participate.

_____

_____

_____

Major Race 3: Leisure Activities

Describe a few notable athletic competitions.

Name: Date:

Notes:

Name: Date:

Notes:

Name: Date:

Notes:

Describe a few notable athletes.

Name: Period Lived:

Notes:

Name: Period Lived:

Notes:

Name: Period Lived:

Notes:

Pets

What creatures are kept as pets?

Who can own pets?

What services are provided by pets?

Where are pets kept?

Where are pets acquired from?

How are pets trained?

How are pets and pet owners treated in society?

Art

How important is art in their society?

_____

What art exists and what are their subjects?

_____

_____

_____

Where did their art originate?

_____

What materials are used to create their art?

_____

_____

_____

What influence has art had on their society?

_____

_____

_____

What special groups of artists exist?

_____

_____

_____

How are artists treated in society?

_____

_____

_____

Describe a few notable pieces of art.

Name: Subject:

Notes:

Name: Subject:

Notes:

Name: Subject:

Notes:

Describe a few notable artists.

Name: Period Lived:

Notes:

Name: Period Lived:

Notes:

Name: Period Lived:

Notes:

Architecture

What materials are used to create their buildings?

_____

_____

_____

Describe their architectural style.

_____

_____

_____

Describe a few common buildings.

Name: Use:
_____

Notes:
_____

_____

Name: Use:
_____

Notes:
_____

_____

Name: Use:
_____

Notes:
_____

_____

Name: Use:
_____

Notes:
_____

_____

Describe a few notable buildings.

Name: Location:
_____
Notes:
_____

_____

_____

Name: Location:
_____
Notes:
_____

_____

_____

Name: Location:
_____
Notes:
_____

_____

_____

Describe a few notable architects.

Name: Period Lived:
_____
Notes:
_____

_____

_____

Name: Period Lived:
_____
Notes:
_____

_____

_____

Name: Period Lived:
_____
Notes:
_____

_____

_____

Major Race 3: Literature

Literature

How common is their ability to read?

_____

How important is literature in their society?

_____

What written records exist and what are their subjects?

_____

_____

_____

What materials are used to record their literature?

_____

_____

_____

What influence has literature had on their society?

_____

_____

_____

What special groups of writers exist?

_____

_____

_____

How are writers treated in society?

_____

_____

_____

Major Race 3: Literature

Describe a few notable pieces of literature.

Name: _____ Subject: _____

Notes: _____

_____

_____

Name: _____ Subject: _____

Notes: _____

_____

_____

Name: _____ Subject: _____

Notes: _____

_____

_____

Describe a few notable authors.

Name: _____ Period Lived: _____

Notes: _____

_____

_____

Name: _____ Period Lived: _____

Notes: _____

_____

_____

Name: _____ Period Lived: _____

Notes: _____

_____

_____

Music

How important is music in their society?

_____

What kinds of music exist and what purpose does music serve?

_____

_____

_____

Where did their music originate?

_____

What instruments are used to create their music?

_____

_____

_____

What influence has music had on their society?

_____

_____

_____

What special groups of musicians exist?

_____

_____

_____

How are musicians treated in society?

_____

_____

_____

Describe a few notable pieces of music.

Name: Subject:

Notes:

Name: Subject:

Notes:

Name: Subject:

Notes:

Describe a few notable musicians.

Name: Period Lived:

Notes:

Name: Period Lived:

Notes:

Name: Period Lived:

Notes:

Major Race 3: Dance

Dance

How important is dance in their society?

_____

What kinds of dances exist and what purpose does dancing serve?

_____

_____

_____

Where did their dance originate?

_____

What outfits, accessories, and props are used during their dances?

_____

_____

_____

What influence has dance had on their society?

_____

_____

_____

What special groups of dancers exist?

_____

_____

_____

How are dancers treated in society?

_____

_____

_____

Describe a few notable dances.

Name: _____   Subject: _____

Notes: _____

_____

_____

Name: _____   Subject: _____

Notes: _____

_____

_____

Name: _____   Subject: _____

Notes: _____

_____

_____

Describe a few notable dancers.

Name: _____   Period Lived: _____

Notes: _____

_____

_____

Name: _____   Period Lived: _____

Notes: _____

_____

_____

Name: _____   Period Lived: _____

Notes: _____

_____

_____

Philosophy

How important is philosophy in their society?

_____

What philosophies exist and what are their subjects?

_____

_____

_____

Where did their philosophies originate?

_____

What methods are used to communicate philosophies?

_____

_____

_____

What influence has philosophy had on their society?

_____

_____

_____

What special groups of philosophers exist?

_____

_____

_____

How are philosophers treated in society?

_____

_____

_____

Describe a few notable philosophies.

Name: _____   Subject: _____

Notes: _____

_____

_____

Name: _____   Subject: _____

Notes: _____

_____

_____

Name: _____   Subject: _____

Notes: _____

_____

_____

Describe a few notable philosophers.

Name: _____   Period Lived: _____

Notes: _____

_____

_____

Name: _____   Period Lived: _____

Notes: _____

_____

_____

Name: _____   Period Lived: _____

Notes: _____

_____

_____

Notes on Major Race 3: _____

Notes on Major Race 3: _____

Major Race 4: _____

Basics

What do they call themselves and what do others call them?

_____

_____

_____

Describe them in three words.

_____   _____   _____

What is the most well-known fact or accepted belief about them?

_____

_____

_____

What is their most guarded secret?

_____

_____

_____

What is the most important part of their society?

_____

_____

_____

_____

Where does most of their population live?

_____

_____   _____

Characteristics

Describe their average physical form.

_____

_____

_____

_____

_____

Draw or paste an image of their average physical form.

Major Race 4: Characteristics

Describe their ideal physical form.

_____

_____

_____

Describe their magical and technological characteristics.

_____

_____

_____

Describe their physical characteristics.

_____

_____

_____

Describe their social characteristics.

_____

_____

_____

Describe their skills and abilities.

_____

_____

_____

Describe their attitude towards other races.

_____

_____

_____

Social Hierarchy

Describe their social hierarchy.

_____

_____

_____

Draw their social hierarchy.

How does an individual's or family's social status affect their daily life?

_____

_____

_____

How can an individual's or family's social status change?

_____

_____

_____

Gender Differences

Describe their genders.

_____

_____

_____

What are the physical differences between genders?

_____

_____

_____

What are the cognitive differences between genders?

_____

_____

_____

What are the perceived and societal gender differences for children?

_____

_____

_____

What are the perceived and societal gender differences for adults?

_____

_____

_____

How do members of different genders commonly interact?

_____

_____

_____

Language

What is the name of the language they speak or sign?

_____

Is the language also written?

_____

Describe how their language sounds and its basic principles.

_____

_____

_____

How and where did their language originate?

_____

_____

_____

How do they communicate with each other?

_____

_____

_____

How do they communicate with other races?

_____

_____

_____

How do they send messages near and far?

_____

_____

_____

Major Race 4: Language

Describe a few common words of their language.

Spoken / Signed Word	Written Word	Translation

Describe a few common phrases of their language.

Spoken / Signed Phrase	Written Phrase	Translation

Names

How are names chosen?

_____

_____

_____

How are names changed?

_____

_____

_____

What significance does a name have on an individual?

_____

_____

_____

How many parts are in a name?

_____

List a few first, female, or other gendered names.

1. _____   5. _____

2. _____   6. _____

3. _____   7. _____

4. _____   8. _____

List a few middle, male, or other gendered names.

1. _____   5. _____

2. _____   6. _____

3. _____   7. _____

4. _____   8. _____

Major Race 4: Names

List a few last, family, or identifying names.

1. _____   6. _____

2. _____   7. _____

3. _____   8. _____

4. _____   9. _____

5. _____   10. _____

List a few titles they can acquire.

Title	Acquired By
1.	
2.	
3.	
4.	
5.	
6.	
7.	
8.	
9.	
10.	
11.	
12.	

Describe how titles may be changed.

_____

_____

_____

Describe the social impact of titles.

_____

_____

_____

Religion

How important is religion in their society? Which religion dominates their culture?

_____

_____

_____

What purpose does religion serve in their society?

_____

_____

_____

What are their beliefs about the beginning of life?

_____

_____

_____

What are their beliefs about death, afterlife, and reincarnation?

_____

_____

_____

Where are how do they practice their religion?

_____

_____

_____

How tolerant of other religious beliefs are they?

_____

_____

_____

Major Race 4: Religion

Describe a few of their deities or important religious individuals.

Name:

Notes:

Name:

Notes:

Name:

Notes:

Name:

Notes:

Name:

Notes:

Name:

Notes:

Describe a few important religious teachings they follow or rituals they perform.

Name:

Notes:

Name:

Notes:

Name:

Notes:

Name:

Notes:

Name:

Notes:

Name:

Notes:

Magic

How important is magic in their society?

_____

What influence has magic had on their society?

_____

_____

_____

What purpose does magic serve in their society?

_____

_____

_____

What do they call their magicians and what do their magicians call themselves?

_____

_____

_____

Describe how they use magic.

_____

_____

_____

Where did their magical knowledge originate?

_____

Who can become a magician?

_____

_____

_____

How are magicians educated?

_____

_____

_____

How are magicians treated in society?

_____

_____

_____

What laws, governing or religious, pertain specifically to magicians?

_____

_____

_____

How do magicians commonly interact with each other?

_____

_____

_____

What special groups of magicians exist?

_____

_____

_____

Describe the hierarchy of magicians.

_____

_____

_____

Major Race 4: Magic

Describe a few notable magicians or spells.

Name:

Notes:

Name:

Notes:

Name:

Notes:

Name:

Notes:

Name:

Notes:

Name:

Notes:

Technology

How important is technology in their society?

What influence has technology had on their society?

What purpose does technology serve in their society?

What do they call their technology, and what do others call it?

Describe how they use technology.

How much of their technology is borrowed or copied from other races?

Who can become an inventor and technology user?

How are inventors and technology users educated?

_____

_____

_____

How are inventors and technology users treated in society?

_____

_____

_____

What laws, governing or religious, pertain specifically to technology users?

_____

_____

_____

_____

How do inventors and technology users commonly interact with each other?

_____

_____

_____

What special groups of inventors and technology users exist?

_____

_____

_____

Describe the hierarchy of inventors and technology users.

_____

_____

_____

Describe a few notable inventors or inventions.

Name:

Notes:

Name:

Notes:

Name:

Notes:

Name:

Notes:

Name:

Notes:

Name:

Notes:

Government

Describe their government.

_____

_____

_____

Who can be a government official?

_____

_____

_____

Who can participate in the government?

_____

_____

_____

What influence does government have in their society?

_____

_____

_____

Describe a few impactful events in the history of their government.

Name: Date:
_____

Notes:
_____

_____

_____

Name: Date:
_____

Notes:
_____

_____

_____

List a few notable laws of their government.

Name: Date Enacted:

Notes:

Name: Date Enacted:

Notes:

Name: Date Enacted:

Notes:

Name: Date Enacted:

Notes:

Name: Date Enacted:

Notes:

Name: Date Enacted:

Notes:

Major Race 4: Government

Describe their foreign policies.

_____
_____
_____

Describe their treaties and alliances.

_____
_____
_____

Describe their rivals and enemies.

_____
_____
_____

Describe a few notable members of their government.

Name: _____ Period Lived: _____

Notes: _____
_____
_____

Name: _____ Period Lived: _____

Notes: _____
_____
_____

Name: _____ Period Lived: _____

Notes: _____
_____
_____

War

Describe their attitude towards war and physical conflicts.

_____

_____

_____

Describe how their society has been affected by war.

_____

_____

_____

Describe a few wars from their history.

Name: Time Period:
_____

Notes:
_____

_____

Name: Time Period:
_____

Notes:
_____

_____

Name: Time Period:
_____

Notes:
_____

_____

Name: Time Period:
_____

Notes:
_____

_____

Major Race 4: War

Describe a few of their weapons and armor.

Name: Material:

Notes:

___

Name: Material:

Notes:

___

Name: Material:

Notes:

___

Describe a few famous warriors and peacekeepers.

Name: Period Lived:

Notes:

___

Name: Period Lived:

Notes:

___

Name: Period Lived:

Notes:

Major Race 4: War

History

How and where did they originate from?

_____

_____

_____

Briefly describe their history.

_____

_____

_____

Describe a few important events in their history.

Name: Date:
_____

Notes:
_____

_____

Name: Date:
_____

Notes:
_____

_____

Name: Date:
_____

Notes:
_____

_____

Name: Date:
_____

Notes:
_____

_____

Achievements

What do they consider their greatest achievement?

_____

_____

_____

What effect have their achievements had on the world?

_____

_____

_____

Describe a few additional achievements they have made.

Name: Date:

Notes:

_____

_____

Name: Date:

Notes:

_____

_____

Name: Date:

Notes:

_____

_____

Name: Date:

Notes:

_____

_____

Economics

What kind of currency is used?

_____

What is their currency made of and what does it look like?

_____

Who monitors and distributes their currency?

_____

_____

_____

What kind of trades can be made?

_____

_____

_____

How is their currency accepted by other races?

_____

_____

_____

Describe a few common valuations.

Item or Service	Trade or Monetary Value
1.	
2.	
3.	
4.	
5.	
6.	
7.	

Major Race 4: Ownership System

Ownership System
What property can be owned?

Who can own property?

What laws and punishments exist regarding stolen and vandalized property?

What happens to property when the owner dies?

Describe slavery within your race and its impact on your world.

Cities

How many cities have they founded?

_____

Where and how were most cities founded?

_____

_____

_____

Describe a few notable cities.

Name: _____ Location: _____

Notes: _____

_____

_____

Name: _____ Location: _____

Notes: _____

_____

_____

Name: _____ Location: _____

Notes: _____

_____

_____

Name: _____ Location: _____

Notes: _____

_____

_____

Housing

In what type of building or area do they live? What is it made of?

_____

_____

_____

Describe how their homes are uniquely adapted to them.

_____

_____

_____

Describe their housing arrangements. Who lives together?

_____

_____

_____

Draw or paste a layout of a common home.

What special housing exists?

_____

_____

_____

Describe how wealth affects housing.

_____

_____

_____

Describe the furniture and items found in their homes.

_____

_____

_____

Draw or paste a layout of a special or wealthy home.

Education

Describe their educational system.

_____

_____

_____

List a few subjects that are taught.

1. _____	9. _____
2. _____	10. _____
3. _____	11. _____
4. _____	12. _____
5. _____	13. _____
6. _____	14. _____
7. _____	15. _____
8. _____	16. _____

Who are the instructors?

_____

_____

_____

Describe their special schools and educational programs.

_____

_____

_____

Who can attend school and who can obtain special education?

_____

_____

_____

Describe a few notable schools.

Name: Location:
_____

Notes:
_____

_____

_____

Name: Location:
_____

Notes:
_____

_____

_____

Name: Location:
_____

Notes:
_____

_____

_____

Describe a few notable educators.

Name: Period Lived:
_____

Notes:
_____

_____

_____

Name: Period Lived:
_____

Notes:
_____

_____

_____

Name: Period Lived:
_____

Notes:
_____

_____

_____

Professions

List a few common professions.

1. _____   5. _____

2. _____   6. _____

3. _____   7. _____

4. _____   8. _____

List a few necessary but uncommon professions.

1. _____   3. _____

2. _____   4. _____

How are professions chosen?

_____

_____

_____

How are professions able to be changed?

_____

_____

_____

How does an individual acquire their professional education?

_____

_____

_____

Describe a few professions and their trade or monetary earnings.

Profession	Trade or Monetary Value
1.	
2.	
3.	

Health

What is the name of their medical practitioners?

_____

Who can be a medical practitioner?

_____

How are medical practitioners educated?

_____

_____

_____

What treatments or medicines are used?

_____

_____

_____

What medical instruments are used?

_____

_____

_____

Does their medicine work on other races?

_____

Describe a few diseases, infections, or sicknesses they can be affected with.

_____

_____

_____

Diet

What does their diet primarily consist of?

How much and how often do they eat?

What utensils are used to prepare and cook food?

What methods is food prepared?

What food sources are gathered?

What food sources are grown or raised?

What food sources are hunted?

What food sources are traded?

Daily Life

Where do they eat?

_____

When are common mealtimes?

_____

Where do they sleep?

_____

When do they sleep and for how long?

_____

What and how do they breathe?

_____

_____

Where and how do they release waste?

_____

_____

Describe their mealtime practices.

_____

_____

_____

Describe their travel arrangements.

_____

_____

_____

Clothing

What are their clothes made of?

What do children wear?

What do adults wear?

What effect does gender have on their clothing?

What accessories do they wear?

What piercings, tattoos or other optional markings can they have?

Describe a few outfits.

Worn By or For:

Notes:

Worn By or For:

Notes:

Worn By or For:

Notes:

Worn By or For:

Notes:

Grooming

How do they groom themselves? How often is it done?

_____

_____

_____

Where do they groom themselves?

_____

_____

_____

How do they view their grooming habits?

_____

_____

_____

How do other races view their grooming habits?

_____

_____

_____

What items are used and what habits are common for female grooming?

_____

_____

_____

What items are used and what habits are common for male grooming?

_____

_____

_____

Children

How are children treated in society?

_____

_____

_____

Who do children reside with?

_____

How are children educated?

_____

_____

_____

Where and with whom do children spend most of their time?

_____

_____

_____

What are a few special events in a child's life?

_____

_____

_____

At what age are children considered to be adolescents?

_____

Describe the experience of becoming an adolescent.

_____

_____

_____

Adolescents

How are adolescents treated in society?

_____

_____

_____

Where and with whom do adolescents spend most of their time?

_____

How are adolescents educated?

_____

_____

What are a few special events in an adolescent's life?

_____

_____

_____

At what age are adolescents considered to be adults?

_____

Describe the physical changes associated with becoming an adult.

_____

_____

_____

Describe the social changes associated with becoming an adult.

_____

_____

_____

Adults

How are adults treated in society?

_____

_____

_____

Where and with whom do adults spend most of their time?

_____

How are adults educated?

_____

_____

What are a few special events in an adult's life?

_____

_____

_____

At what age are adults considered to be elderly?

_____

Describe the physical changes associated with becoming elderly.

_____

_____

_____

Describe the social changes associated with becoming elderly.

_____

_____

_____

The Elderly

How are the elderly treated in society?

_____

_____

_____

What special treatments exist to honor the elderly?

_____

_____

Where and with whom do the elderly spend most of their time?

_____

_____

_____

What are a few special events in an elder's life?

_____

_____

_____

At what age do the elderly die?

_____

What ways exist to reverse the aging process or prolong the life of the elderly?

_____

_____

What influence do they elderly have on society?

_____

_____

_____

Etiquette

What is the proper relationship between the young and the elderly?

_____

_____

_____

What is the proper relationship between child and parent?

_____

_____

_____

What is the proper relationship between siblings?

_____

_____

_____

Describe a few examples of proper etiquette.

Situation:

_____

Acceptable Etiquette:

_____

_____

Situation:

_____

Acceptable Etiquette:

_____

_____

Situation:

_____

Acceptable Etiquette:

_____

_____

Major Race 4: Death

Death

What ritual is performed after death?

_____

_____

_____

Who participates in the ritual?

_____

_____

_____

What happens to the corpse of the dead?

_____

_____

_____

In what ways are the dead honored or remembered?

_____

_____

_____

How does death affect society and an individual's family?

_____

_____

_____

List the most common causes of death.

1. _____ 5. _____

2. _____ 6. _____

3. _____ 7. _____

4. _____ 8. _____

Courtship & Marriage

How are potential partners selected for courtship?

_____

_____

How is courtship initiated?

_____

_____

Describe the process of courtship.

_____

_____

_____

What is it called to be married?

_____

Under what governing law or ceremony can individuals marry and is it for life?

_____

_____

Describe the events that come before the ceremony and interactions between the individuals.

_____

_____

_____

Describe the marriage ceremony.

_____

_____

_____

Major Race 4: Courtship & Marriage

What are the social effects of marriage on the individuals?

_____

_____

_____

What are the social effects of marriage on the individuals' families?

_____

_____

_____

Describe the religious or government laws of marriage.

_____

_____

_____

Under what circumstances can the religious or governmental marriage laws be broken?

_____

_____

_____

What are the social effects on individuals if the religious or governmental marriage law is broken?

_____

_____

_____

If a married individual dies can the surviving partner(s) participate in a new marriage ceremony?

_____

_____

_____

Reproduction

At what age do they reach sexual maturity and gain the ability to reproduce?

_____

At what age does reproduction stop?

_____

Do they mate with only one partner or have multiple partners?

_____

How are mates chosen?

_____

_____

Which genders can reproduce and how is it done?

_____

_____

_____

How often do they reproduce and how many children are born at a time?

_____

How long does pregnancy last?

_____

What are the physical, emotional, and social effects of pregnancy on an individual?

_____

_____

_____

_____

Major Race 4: Reproduction

What are the social effects of pregnancy on the pregnant individual's partner(s) and their families?

_____

_____

_____

What methods are used to prevent pregnancy?

_____

_____

What methods are used to encourage pregnancy?

_____

_____

What methods are used to terminate a pregnancy?

_____

_____

What are the social effects of a terminated pregnancy?

_____

_____

Describe the birthing process. Who assist with the process?

_____

_____

_____

_____

What are common risks associated with birth?

_____

_____

What other races can they reproduce with?

_____

What is the result of a child conceived by a member of this race and another race?

_____

_____

_____

What differences occur in a pregnancy of a child conceived between a member of this race and another race?

_____

_____

What differences occur in the birth of a child conceived between a member of this race and another race?

_____

_____

What role does government and religion have in reproduction?

_____

_____

_____

What role does magic and technology have in reproduction?

_____

_____

_____

What is the social effect of reproduction occurring outside of marriage?

_____

_____

Special Occasions

List a few special occasions they observe.

1.	8.
2.	9.
3.	10.
4.	11.
5.	12.
6.	13.
7.	14.

Describe a few special occasions they observe.

Name: Date:

Notes:

Name: Date:

Notes:

Name: Date:

Notes:

Name: Date:

Notes:

Leisure Activities

What leisure activities are enjoyed by children?

_____

_____

_____

What leisure activities are enjoyed by adolescents?

_____

_____

_____

What leisure activities are enjoyed by adults?

_____

_____

_____

What leisure activities are enjoyed by the elderly?

_____

_____

_____

Describe leisure sports that are played and who can participate.

_____

_____

_____

Describe competitive sports that are played and who can participate.

_____

_____

_____

Major Race 4: Leisure Activities

Describe a few notable athletic competitions.

Name: Date:
_____
Notes:
_____
_____
_____

Name: Date:
_____
Notes:
_____
_____
_____

Name: Date:
_____
Notes:
_____
_____
_____

Describe a few notable athletes.

Name: Period Lived:
_____
Notes:
_____
_____
_____

Name: Period Lived:
_____
Notes:
_____
_____
_____

Name: Period Lived:
_____
Notes:
_____
_____
_____

Pets

What creatures are kept as pets?

_____

_____

_____

Who can own pets?

_____

_____

What services are provided by pets?

_____

_____

_____

Where are pets kept?

_____

_____

_____

Where are pets acquired from?

_____

How are pets trained?

_____

_____

How are pets and pet owners treated in society?

_____

_____

_____

Major Race 4: Art

Art

How important is art in their society?

What art exists and what are their subjects?

Where did their art originate?

What materials are used to create their art?

What influence has art had on their society?

What special groups of artists exist?

How are artists treated in society?

Describe a few notable pieces of art.

Name: _____ Subject: _____

Notes: _____

_____

_____

Name: _____ Subject: _____

Notes: _____

_____

_____

Name: _____ Subject: _____

Notes: _____

_____

_____

Describe a few notable artists.

Name: _____ Period Lived: _____

Notes: _____

_____

_____

Name: _____ Period Lived: _____

Notes: _____

_____

_____

Name: _____ Period Lived: _____

Notes: _____

_____

_____

Architecture

What materials are used to create their buildings?

_____

_____

_____

Describe their architectural style.

_____

_____

_____

Describe a few common buildings.

Name: Use:
Notes:
_____

_____

_____

Name: Use:
Notes:
_____

_____

_____

Name: Use:
Notes:
_____

_____

_____

Name: Use:
Notes:
_____

_____

_____

Describe a few notable buildings.

Name: _____ Location: _____

Notes: _____

_____

_____

Name: _____ Location: _____

Notes: _____

_____

_____

Name: _____ Location: _____

Notes: _____

_____

_____

Describe a few notable architects.

Name: _____ Period Lived: _____

Notes: _____

_____

_____

Name: _____ Period Lived: _____

Notes: _____

_____

_____

Name: _____ Period Lived: _____

Notes: _____

_____

_____

Literature

How common is their ability to read?

How important is literature in their society?

What written records exist and what are their subjects?

What materials are used to record their literature?

What influence has literature had on their society?

What special groups of writers exist?

How are writers treated in society?

Describe a few notable pieces of literature.

Name: Subject:

Notes:

Name: Subject:

Notes:

Name: Subject:

Notes:

Describe a few notable authors.

Name: Period Lived:

Notes:

Name: Period Lived:

Notes:

Name: Period Lived:

Notes:

Music

How important is music in their society?

_____

What kinds of music exist and what purpose does music serve?

_____

_____

Where did their music originate?

_____

What instruments are used to create their music?

_____

_____

What influence has music had on their society?

_____

_____

What special groups of musicians exist?

_____

_____

How are musicians treated in society?

_____

_____

Describe a few notable pieces of music.

Name: Subject:

Notes:

Name: Subject:

Notes:

Name: Subject:

Notes:

Describe a few notable musicians.

Name: Period Lived:

Notes:

Name: Period Lived:

Notes:

Name: Period Lived:

Notes:

Dance

How important is dance in their society?

_____

What kinds of dances exist and what purpose does dancing serve?

_____

_____

_____

Where did their dance originate?

_____

What outfits, accessories, and props are used during their dances?

_____

_____

_____

What influence has dance had on their society?

_____

_____

_____

What special groups of dancers exist?

_____

_____

_____

How are dancers treated in society?

_____

_____

_____

Describe a few notable dances.

Name: Subject:

Notes:

Name: Subject:

Notes:

Name: Subject:

Notes:

Describe a few notable dancers.

Name: Period Lived:

Notes:

Name: Period Lived:

Notes:

Name: Period Lived:

Notes:

Philosophy

How important is philosophy in their society?

_____

What philosophies exist and what are their subjects?

_____

_____

_____

Where did their philosophies originate?

_____

What methods are used to communicate philosophies?

_____

_____

_____

What influence has philosophy had on their society?

_____

_____

_____

What special groups of philosophers exist?

_____

_____

_____

How are philosophers treated in society?

_____

_____

_____

Describe a few notable philosophies.

Name: _____ Subject: _____

Notes: _____

_____

_____

Name: _____ Subject: _____

Notes: _____

_____

_____

Name: _____ Subject: _____

Notes: _____

_____

_____

Describe a few notable philosophers.

Name: _____ Period Lived: _____

Notes: _____

_____

_____

Name: _____ Period Lived: _____

Notes: _____

_____

_____

Name: _____ Period Lived: _____

Notes: _____

_____

_____

Notes on Major Race 4: _____

Notes on Major Race 4: _____

Minor Race 1: _____

What do they call themselves and what do others call them?

_____

_____

How large is their population and where do they live?

_____

Describe them in three words.

_____ _____ _____

Describe their physical appearance.

_____

_____

_____

Describe their personalities.

_____

_____

_____

Describe their culture.

_____

_____

_____

_____

_____

What language do they speak, write, or sign?

_____ _____

What are some of their names?

Describe their use of magic.

Describe their use of technology.

Describe their government.

Describe their religion.

Describe their relationships with other races.

Minor Race 2: _____

What do they call themselves and what do others call them?

_____

_____

How large is their population and where do they live?

_____

Describe them in three words.

_____ _____ _____

Describe their physical appearance.

_____

_____

_____

Describe their personalities.

_____

_____

_____

Describe their culture.

_____

_____

_____

_____

_____

What language do they speak, write, or sign?

_____

What are some of their names?

_____

_____

_____

Describe their use of magic.

_____

_____

_____

Describe their use of technology.

_____

_____

_____

Describe their government.

_____

_____

_____

Describe their religion.

_____

_____

_____

Describe their relationships with other races.

_____

_____

_____

_____

_____

Minor Race 3: _____

What do they call themselves and what do others call them?

_____

_____

How large is their population and where do they live?

_____

Describe them in three words.

_____ _____ _____

Describe their physical appearance.

_____

_____

_____

Describe their personalities.

_____

_____

_____

Describe their culture.

_____

_____

_____

_____

_____

What language do they speak, write, or sign?

_____

What are some of their names?

Describe their use of magic.

Describe their use of technology.

Describe their government.

Describe their religion.

Describe their relationships with other races.

Minor Race 4: _____

What do they call themselves and what do others call them?

_____

_____

How large is their population and where do they live?

_____

Describe them in three words.

_____   _____   _____

Describe their physical appearance.

_____

_____

_____

Describe their personalities.

_____

_____

_____

Describe their culture.

_____

_____

_____

_____

_____

What language do they speak, write, or sign?

_____

What are some of their names?

Describe their use of magic.

Describe their use of technology.

Describe their government.

Describe their religion.

Describe their relationships with other races.

Notes on Minor Races

Additional Notes

Additional Notes

Additional Notes

Additional Notes

Additional Notes

Additional Notes

Additional Notes

Additional Notes

Additional Notes

Additional Notes

Additional Notes

Made in the USA
Middletown, DE
13 June 2023

32529796R00223